Archelon Ranch

by

Garrett Cook

LegumeMan Books

Published in Australia by LegumeMan Books
info@legumeman.com
www.legumeman.com
Copyright © Garrett Cook 2009
The moral right of this author has been asserted.
Art copyright © Jude Coulter-Pultz - judebook.deviantart.com

Typeset in Dustismo Roman Copyright © 2002 Dustin Norlander
http://www.cheapskatefonts.com:

ISBN: 978-0-9805938-2-2

*favorite song
They play it once again, they
play it all night long..."*

- The Talking Heads,
  Heaven

*...know not,
Am I my brother's keeper?"*

- Genesis, 4:9

I

Je ne suis pas un chapeau. Je suis un homme. Je ne suis pas un chapeau. Je suis un homme. Je suis un homme. Je ne suis pas un chapeau. Je suis un homme. He speaks, repeating these words, but the news vendor does not understand at all. The man beneath him whose very head he sits upon does not understand at all. What's there to understand? Je ne suis pas un chapeau. Je suis un homme. Je ne suis pas un chapeau! How is it said? Parlez-vous français, monsieur? Parlez-vous français? Je ne parle pas anglais. Parlez-vous français monsieur? Je ne suis pas un chapeau. Je suis un homme!

The news vendor scratched his head and gave the man wearing Bernard a very dirty look, as if he were clearly up to something awful.

"What's with your hat, pal? Are you up to some-thin'? Is this some bullshit Ministry of Morale gag? If it is, it ain't funny."

"It's been saying that all day." The man's voice was extremely contrite. He didn't speak any French …only English. Bernard's psyche relaxed, expanded and found the language. Within moments, he remembered English.

"I am not a hat," Bernard said very slowly and matter-of-factly. "I am a man."

He was, of course, a hat. He was a grey felt fedora, pure Dashiell Hammett, on the head of an overweight used car salesman whose name lurked somewhere in there, somewhere behind the English. First soak up the form, then the content. That's how it worked. Bernard was relieved that the news vendor was looking right at him instead of down at the salesman.

"I'm sorry, son," the news vendor's voice got low, full of lament, "but I'm afraid you're a hat. Whatever else you might be or think you are, you're a hat my friend."

He wished he had little felt fists to pound the man's head and little felt legs to run off, but as a hat, he had neither. The hat struggled long and hard to get off of the man and Bernard struggled long and hard to stop being a hat. The head was a box for the hat. The hat was a box for Bernard. He struggled with boxes within boxes, like a six year old recipient of a christmas prank.

The man was named Howard Schultz. He sold cars for a living, which was hard to make much money doing, what with traffic being what it was and the city being what it was: dangerous, expensive, real tough to make a living. Howard was considering getting out of the game. Bernard, who decided it might somehow be better to be the hat than to be Howard Schultz, felt like that might be a good idea, though he was just getting reacquainted with the concept of used car sales via osmosis.

"I'm not a hat..."

"I don't need this today, hat. First you, and then next thing you know my pants are tryin' to tell me what's what. I won't have it."

"My name is..."

Before Bernard could finish this very significant thought, a chimpanzee descended from the great canopy above and removed him from Howard

Schultz's head, carrying him up into the massive, overgrown gingko that towered over and grew into the car salesman's apartment building. The chimps had developed an interest in hats and were known to take them from those who wore them and play with them until more interesting headgear could be found. The chimp sported Bernard proudly before the other, less fashionable, monkeys in the treetops, who looked much less chic in their visors, baseball hats and thick sunglasses. They powwowed in a circle, exchanging grunts and screeches over the newfound treasure, which impressed the other monkeys a lot.

"I'm not a hat," Bernard repeated, but the monkeys no more understood English than the news vendor understood French. He reached into the monkey for their language, but it was harder, so he decided he would talk to the other hats instead. Like most inanimate objects, they understood their own kind through telepathic signals and subtle electrical impulses, little blips of existential shock. When chairs speak to chairs, for example, they say "I am a chair and this is true", as things must know their own. The assertions must be made and they must claim the attention of the prospective listener.

"I am a hat and I am not a hat," went the message and the other hats echoed their reply in unison. "I am a hat and you are definitely wrong," it went, but somehow they could tell that the new hat was right on some level. This upset them, because it was very hard to grasp and the thought that maybe they too weren't hats was offensive and scary.

"I am a hat and I am not a hat," Bernard, the hat, repeated. This time the others did not respond. Bernard struggled as a hat once more to escape the tyranny of the chimp's head and as Bernard to escape the tyranny of having to live as a hat. He was sure he knew, however distantly, what it was like to be as Howard Schultz and the news vendor were: walking around, buying and selling newspapers, choosing what hat they would wear. He decided that Howard Schultz, car salesman or otherwise, was lucky and that he too had once been so lucky. He was now, however, a hat. The news vendor had said he was a hat and the chimp was wearing him as a hat. Bernard was a gray, felt fedora. I am a hat and I am not a hat. I am a hat and I am a hat. The other hats around him appreciated it a lot. Gray felt beingness; a singular sense of purpose. There was no further need to communicate between them, as they had nothing much to say to each other; no need to discuss at length the contours of heads and the feeling that nothing was expected of them. If it were not for the fan blades that floated even above the treetops, Bernard would have spent quite awhile thinking of nothing more than life as a gray felt fedora.

The blades spun fast and the few people below wearing hats hung onto them tightly. Mothers assumed iron grips on their strollers as the wind that cooled the city blew hard, fast and cold. The temperature became a cool, crisp one hundred and five degrees, almost the weather for cargo shorts or a light skirt, the heaviest clothes people bothered to wear in the city. Bernard heard the collective sigh below as he, like every other hat, was swept up in the wind.

The last time he had felt flight was inside a rhamphoryncus, a leathery dragonbird that came down from a nest atop the control tower on the platform to feast on chimp flesh and that of a couple of harvesters. The harvesters were hard to eat, but delicious, at least for a carnivorous pterosaur. As a hat, he watched harvesters fight off the monkeys and the man-eating dinosaurs to get at the ripe, bluegreen fruits on the top branches. Their skin, engineered to endure the sun beating down hard, was jet black and covered by thick shells. Other than that, they were just people like Bernard and tasted like people.

If he had never been the pterosaur, he would never have thought that human flesh could be edible, and especially wouldn't have thought that about harvester flesh. He wished that there was a way for hats to eat, since his time as a hat was beginning to corrode his sense of decency and human propriety and had thus rendered the harvesters appetizing.

He begged himself to stop. Harvesters were people. Bernard was Bernard and Bernard was people as well. His humanity hit him hard and fast as he felt moved; moved and saddened as people walked out of their homes and workplaces to take in the three o'clock breeze. The jaguars, most of the oviraptors and even the dreaded gilawalrus instinctually came out of their places in alleys and urban underbrush to hunt when the wind came, since their prey would be distracted, plentiful and brazen. The police cars and civic triceratops couldn't stop every one of them, even if they tried and focused their energy on the wealthier boroughs where spoiled, overfed tyrannosaurs, kept as pets and guardbeasts by local fatcats, had gone rogue. People below him were not safe, not as safe as a hat, whose only natural predator was moths. For a moment, it was worth the risk for them, a moment to feel skin under the salt was a moment of actual living... They went so far as to enlist the aid of other beasts to survive, bringing out komodo dragons, king cobras and hadrosaurs to defend them against the hungry jungle cats and beady-eyed baby gobbling vermin though of course, they had yet to find a match for the gilawalrus.

In spite of the cut-rate reptilian bodyguards, the people of the city did not cool off in peace. There was a tornado of spots, claws, neon stripes and animal screeches. Blood, blood, blood. Mothers cried for their babies unprotected from the heat by the voodoo thermostats inside, pure superstition that couldn't stand up to the sun. Air conditioning was a joke, an archaism of the highest order; mandatory, but a joke.

The only hope each day was of course the wind and it saddened Bernard deeply how much people paid for it. He wished that hats had eyes so he could cry.

He embraced the freedom of flight on the wind until he landed, and where he landed was squarely on the head of Rebecca Inez Takahashi, a first grade teacher who wore a pale blue thong and sparkly pasties. She was about thirty pounds overweight, but couldn't bring herself to care. Rebecca wished that society would just acknowledge that nudity was a must in this hot, sticky, terrible world. She cheered up a little and a smile crossed her face when Bernard landed on her head. She felt glamorous, a little mischievous too. She felt like pulling off her pasties and removing her thong so she could be naked with just her silly, new, gray felt hat on. But, as was her way, she kept her exhibitionist fantasy to herself and did not subject the rest of the street to its consequences. But, it would be so nice... She preened and modeled her new hat and the people catching the breeze watched as she did.

The hadrosaurs and komodo dragons looked to and fro, but the raptors weren't abroad on Fourth Street and the Fourth Street jaguars had decided that starvation would be better than enduring the punishments dished out by the hard heads of the duck-billed dinosaurs or the great bulk of a komodo dragon pouncing upon them. On this day, Fourth Street relaxed, for the most part.

Relaxed, that was, until one of THOSE THINGS arrived. The hadrosaurs growled low and strained on their leashes, able to recognize the threat the fairly humanoid creature that walked down the street posed. This "man" was not shirtless, nor did he wear denim cut-offs or a speedo. This "man" was dressed in a thick, beige overcoat with a white dress shirt and neatly pressed pants. This "man" carried an umbrella, although it was not one of the scheduled precipitation days. From the slightly green tint of his skin and the hard, clumpy chunks of green vomit running down his chin, it was clear that this was a Suburbanite. If hats could tremble, Bernard would have.

"Give me back my hat, cocksuckers! I need my lucky cocksucking hat, cocksuckers!" it shrieked.

Before Rebecca Inez Takahashi could say anything or relinquish the hat (which she was certainly not willing to die for), the Suburbanite was upon her, biting a hole in her throat. As she bled to death, the Suburbanite fell to his knees and wept bitterly, making an awful, inhuman sound with his throat; the gurgling sound of the mud churning and coming up. Bernard looked on from the top of the dead woman's head watching the disgusting spectacle of the Suburbanite crying, screeching and vomiting green mud.

"I want my lucky cocksucking hat, you cocksucker!" the Suburbanite once more wailed. The citizens stared at the abomination and couldn't help but wonder why they still let those things roam free.

"Disgusting!" said one of the citizens, who was almost run down by a police cruiser remote dispatched to the scene. The cruiser needed only to open its door before she grudgingly got in, not wanting anymore trouble for her intolerant outburst. With a blaze of the cruiser's side-mounted machine guns, the Suburbanite and the body of Rebecca Inez Takahashi were both perforated to shreds. As was, for the most part, the grey fedora that was Bernard. As death pulled at him, he pulled away.

Falling through the dust tunnel, he came out the other end. Heaven and Hell had no objections, as always. So, as always, he came out and found the bed, where his father and Professor Sagramore stood over him anxiously.

"Deep Objectivity," Professor Sagramore declared, "I hate to say it, but the side effects are catching up."

"But he isn't a Suburbanite."

"We've done better than that. Transcended it."

"More CRAMPS? Should we give him extra injections?"

"Absolutely. You know what I say about extra injections."

Bernard's father plunged the syringe into him, but it did little good. Bernard was already gone again. Deep Objectivity caught up to subjects quickly.

He wandered the city, a new tyrannosaurus devouring innocent people, pedestrians and irate hadrosaurs. When the police triceratops came around, he tussled hard, but he came out on top, feasting on the delicious innards of his foe. This stirred something in the back of Bernard's saurian brain, revealing something strange and fantastic; a message, an image. There was a place out there, thick with foliage like the city, but different. There was but one building, made up of marble, tended by smiling, nude golden haired ladies and surrounded by fruit trees which grew into a sky, blue as any ocean, though that could not be said since the secret place overlooked an ocean which was bluer than any other, bluer than any sky or any ocean could be. Great sea turtles, ancient perhaps as the earth itself and wearing contented, wise expressions on their leathery faces swam in this ocean.

"The Archelon Ranch is calling you," a voice said over the message, "the Archelon Ranch is calling you home. Primal and beautiful man, come home, you are welcome once again."

But, like all the other journeys into deeper Objectivity, this one ended with Bernard coming back to the bed, eyes wide, heart hungry. Archelon Ranch is calling me home. I am welcome once again.

II

Angry, sopping wet, covered in amniotic ink, I crawled through gaps in the narrative and I was born. I was a near accident before I was tossed aside, an additional piece of background on a protagonist who did not need to be that three-dimensional. Did Bernard really need a family? Did Bernard need a favorite cereal, a favorite novel, a favorite anything? How much Bernard did there need to be? But, as my relevance waned, I screamed, I made my presence known. It can be done. Anything can Assert itself if it needs to. The cereal, Vitaboom, could have argued itself more persuasively into being and this book could have opened with the scene of Bernard at the breakfast table (where he seldom was) crunching loudly (as he tended to) and slurping down his milk, blue with synthberry proteins. By assertion, Vitaboom could have made itself incredibly relevant. Bernard could have discovered that Vitaboom was made from the eggs of some hypnotic space reptile, seeking to make the Earth vulnerable to suggestions from the nefarious Space Iguana hive mind. Vitaboom is made from soy and perfectly common birdeating spider eggs, but it could be quite important if it had only longed to be. His "Voluntary Necrosis" t-shirt could spangle its gangrenous limbs across every scene Bernard appears in. But it didn't, which I guess is okay because Bernard really wasn't all that into the music of Voluntary Necrosis. He doesn't listen to music. Favorite novel couldn't assert itself because Bernard is really not the reading type. He has the complete works of Jack London stored in his memory as a side-effect of his genetic splicing, but he didn't really look at it much. Outside of his special condition, Bernard was a person who would be of little interest to anybody. And yet...boils my blood!

I guess my life wasn't all that special either at the beginning. I spent my days at a dinosaur pesticide warehouse in the raptor spray department. Some work. Mix the contents of tank A with tank B; filter out toxic materials into tank C. Bring tank C to inner city middle schools where I sell it as a Nitrus Oxide substitute. The real function of this is to stifle intellectual growth so none of these children end up proving government studies regarding their inferiority incorrect. Then, I would go home and watch the sixteen year old nymphette across the street masturbate through the lens of my telescopic megawebcam, edit the best material, put it together with the scenes of her fucking her nanny that I taped on weekends and embed it chemically into liquifilm injections which I would sell at the Mall. I of course went armed, because you never know when Suburbanites could wander in unnoticed and get you. It was a stable life, I guess, providing the requisite funds to buy the liquifilm I craved and the imported beers I liked best. Neoxanadu dark rice is 188 proof and it only took three to put me into an eight hour drunken coma, averting eight whole hours of dealing with scorching heat and urban chaos. When I needed extra money, I would kill the orangutans on the Hendersons' roof. At least I would pretend to, since the orangs and I had a great deal going where I would trade them bananas and heroin for Rolex watches and fried chicken.

Not stable. Pathetic. Deviant. I wish Bernard liked me, but I just wasn't his kind of guy. When the Church of Authorial Intent went public after years of being a secret society, I felt like I could change that. Most people snickered, thinking Narrativists had a collective screw loose. Silly Calvino bullshit. Mad, careening postmodern cluelessness. But, I read the pamphlets. After looking them over, I brought them down to Bernard's "room" in the basement to share a secret. From what I knew of Garrett Cook (little though it was, as he was not a frequently published writer) from the excerpts and the Authorial Intent lectures, I discovered that Bernard was quite likely the Protagonist. A lonely, quiet, mentally ill young man possessing godlike psychic potential had to be it. Bernard didn't buy it. I told him that if he wanted to, he could fix all of this and get us out of here safe and sound, but he didn't buy it.

"Why would anybody do this to me?" he asked from behind the plexiglass.

As a perpetual test subject, Bernard permanently existed in a fog of self pity. I hoped that he would be able to emerge from it, for if he didn't, why then... then... then...

I scanned the Authorial Intent pamphlets and came out with no answers about Bernard save the standard 9th grade English/ John Gardner's Art of Fiction explanation. Conflict would cause Bernard to develop. One would think that being Sagramore's guinea pig for twenty four years would be sufficient conflict to develop Bernard. Being allowed upstairs only for his bowl of Vitaboom and his trip to the community pool should have been conflict, which should have been, according to door-to-door Camp-bellians, his call to adventure. This wasn't enough for Bernard. I might have doubted that Bernard was the protagonist at all had it not been for the things that Authorial Intent had taught me about Garrett Cook. Garrett Cook suffered from claustrophobia, a wounded animus, dubious sense of self and intense positive and negative reinforcement alike during his school years. Bernard carried a sense of self pity that Authorial Intent would refuse to attribute to Garrett Cook, but was clearly present in some of his collected online art community blogs from his early twenties. It made me wish I could have sent out for a better author. Maybe one with a bigger, more mainstream audience to reign in the gore and explicit sexuality that the sadistic young pervert splattered all over his work. It's not that I dislike sex and violence, it's just that I worry about cannibal hookers and deadly sex droids. How could I feel safe?

One time I tried to talk to my father about Authorial Intent. It was the day after I first told Bernard he might be the Protagonist and he gave his very disappointing reaction.

"What's going on, Clyde?" my father asked, seeing that I was a picture of concern. I named myself Clyde because Garrett Cook did not give me a name. I think it was because of the orangutans and a Clint Eastwood movie the author once saw. It was floating out there and I simply grabbed it and claimed it for my own. I may have named myself after a monkey, but we live in a world of many, many monkeys.

"I think Bernard might be the Protagonist."

His eyes lit up, which was peculiar, because my father's eyes do not light up often.

"Ah, Authorial Intent! Plot preserve!"

"Plot preserve."

"I considered raising you boys as Narrativists, but your mother wouldn't have it."

Garrett Cook simply forgot outright to create our mother, although he knew that she was something of a fussbudget. My mother, as a result, had no distinguishing features other than an apron she occasionally wore to bake things. Throughout my life, there was no sign of her, more or less, since she either died or divorced my father due to his godless experiments on Bernard.

My father put his hand on his chin and lit his pipe.

"So, you're saying that Bernard's the Protagonist?"

"Yes." My heart felt like loaf of stale bread as I said it.

"No. I don't think it's likely. No author would bother to make something so wretched and unimpressive as Bernard the protagonist of a book, even a short one. It's not really done. Bernard's just a test subject, though I must admit I have been grooming him for Antagonism. He has great psychic potential and I imagine all sorts of awful neuroses from being locked in the basement like that."

"I don't think he's got Antagonism in him."

"Well, he's definitely not a suitable protagonist. I imagine he wants nothing more than—"

So, I laid it on the table.

"I think perhaps we should treat him better."

"That's not like you. Just yesterday you did his injections yourself!"

"I was jealous."

My father puffed harder on his pipe. My father did nothing but smoke his pipe and oversee the injections. Unlike me and certain others, my father never aspired to a life outside the narrative.

"As well you should be if this halfbaked theory of yours turns out to be true. Something pretty incredible would have to happen for him to make our lives any better and I feel no distinct urge to let him try. Although that might just be because that's what the narrative wants from me. After all, something incredible must happen. As a Narrativist, I must have faith in such things. There will be a Protagonist someday, I assure you, and he'll be tough and redemptive with lots of real answers. Maybe Bernard's some sort of pathetic lab monkey sidekick he's supposed to rescue."

I abandoned the conversation, letting my father continue with his lung melting idleness and the crushing boredom that he endured between injections. It would be particularly hard on him now since Bernard had already had his injections for the day.

Later that day, Bernard began speaking through the bedside table. My father was ecstatic, knowing that the boy was starting to experience Objectivity. If successfully harnessed, Bernard's Objectivity had no end of viable corporate and scientific uses. The capacity to speak to nuclear missiles and tell them to go back home, for one thing, would change warfare forever. This made me even more jealous of Bernard.

That day, as I mixed the raptor poison and sold off the remainder of the tank, I had to wonder whether I was part of the problem or not. I dismissed my doubts, and yet I still gave those kids twenty percent off. I was somewhat of a nice guy. I had lobbied for Bernard's comfort and I had helped the inner city's economic squeeze. Later on, I did wince at the irony that three of those children, high on raptor gas, wandered into the street and were devoured by raptors. Life in this city was tough. We needed a hero and our hero was possibly locked in my basement.

As many people do when a crisis of conscience comes around, I attended church for the first time. The sermon was on proper behavior for extras in a bar fight scene, which raised many a question: How many should beset the Protagonist at once? Was it fair for the bartender to reach for his shotgun before the hero had knocked down half of the assailants coming at him? Was it fair for the biggest guy in the room to throw a sucker punch? Could more than one person in the bar fight pull nunchaku, whips or similar exotic weapons to add tension and the illusion of expertise? The Reverend John Calvin Jenkins addressed these points one at a time, going over the Narrativist relevance of each one more meticulously than the last. The sermon lasted four and a half hours and somehow I was captivated by every minute of it. I never watched a John Wayne movie the same way after that (not that I watched John Wayne movies very often as Westerns had a tendency to have viruses in the liquifilm and it wasn't a risk I felt was worth taking).

As the crowd thinned out, I approached the Reverend and introduced myself. He said nothing to me, but he did lead me into his office.

"You're Bernard's brother," said the Reverend, polishing the gold semicolon around his neck as he spoke, "there are theories."

"There are theories? So I'm not the only one then?"

"As a Narrativist, you should know that almost no ideas are original. Of course you're not the only one to have thought of Bernard as a possible Protagonist. But I don't think it's likely. I don't know Bernard myself, but I've heard he just sits in a tiny cell in the basement being poked and prodded and experimented. Nothing special about a guy like that. Too damaged. Too frayed. Too pessimistic. We live in a better world than that."

I had heard this argument before, and didn't feel like having any part of it. I was a man who mixed raptor poison for a living, making money on the side by selling drugs to monkeys on a nearby rooftop. We lived in a huge city defended only by enormous malls on all sides, plagued by dinosaurs, jungle cats, snakes and unruly apes. We needed automated police cruisers and triceratops to keep our streets even close to clean. The suburbs were full of oozing, green hallucinogenic mud that turned all its citizens into maladjusted homicidal maniacs, and god knows what was beyond the suburbs. We live in a better world than that? I felt like spitting in his face for saying it, but the sermon showed he understood the flow somewhat. The deep cosmic awareness he had shown must have been tainted by an unnecessary optimism. He needed something to take the edge off the existential bleakness native to Authorial Intent. That something was the thing that bothers me about every religion and I guess the best thing about them: faith. I had a backhanded, cynical sort of faith in my brother.

"Considering what I see every time I walk down the street, I don't know if I can say that this is too good of a world for Bernard. Seems like you haven't been paying any attention."

The reverend was deathly silent. He reached into the pocket of his red, silk priest robe for a comb, which he ran through his thick, Einstein hairdo. He removed his pink shades so he could look me straight in the eyes, which he did with a passion and venom that I had seen in very few men indeed. But, I stood my ground. At this point, most people would have walked out of the office and gone home. I'm rude and stubborn, though. One of those traits was written into me, the other I developed to survive.

"Reverend, Bernard is the Protagonist."

"You're deluding yourself. It makes no sense."

"If Bernard is the protagonist, is there anything I can do for him?"

"If Bernard is the protagonist, we're all completely and utterly fucked."

"But what should I do?"

The Reverend didn't want to think about it, but he did ponder the situation.

"For starters, Bernard is locked in your basement. You might want to start there, since I don't think he's capable of much heroism where he is. But, I'm not sure you're relevant enough to rescue him, which gives me even less faith in him as a candidate."

I seethed. I ached. My body trembled with the urge to bite, scratch and pound him and, by doing so, to show him just how relevant I could be. By the virtue of surviving I would be the more important of our violent tussle. I hated his words even more, because I had seen how right he was, and seen the people

Acknowledgements

To Leza, for letting me be myself and loving me for who I am, thanks for five years. To the Bizarro community, especially Jeff, Cameron, Andy, Jordan, Rose and Eckhard, for letting me be myself and loving me for who I am in a more platonic way. Thanks for one year. To Jeremy Needle at ENE for knowing that you don't need a weatherman to know which way the wind blows. To the Brothers Gunther and the Minx. for deciding that this jungle nightmare deserved to grow tall and wind its vines around the Earth. To tyrannosaurus rex for being the avatar of my bathtime wrath (my brathtime?). To everybody who stood beside and everybody who stabbed me in the back thank you. Shampoo for my real friends and real poo for my sham friends. To Jude for understanding me enough to create a kickass cover that might just be the reason this book is in your hand. To Toho, Burroughs, Stan Lee, Jack Kirby and Ray Harryhausen. To my family and the basement thing. But not whatever was in the attic. I'm tired. That was a lot. Shit, you'd think people were gonna read this.

Other titles by Garrett Cook

Murderland Part 1: H8
Murderland Part 2: Life During Wartime
Jimmy Plush: Teddybear Detective (coming soon)

on the streets, shuffling back and forth, waiting to get either eaten or rescued from being eaten. The Narrativists did this fairly often, developing hobbies and ways of life that contributed to the plot and milieu without disrupting it. They had made themselves relevant by building colorful saloons, gaudy nightclubs and shops that sold things like shotguns and exorcism manuals which would be useful to the protagonist of a Cook novel. They created homey little restaurants where other Narrativists hung out solely for atmosphere, desperate actors martyring themselves to their elaborate sets. I went on with my life after finding out about Authorial Intent and it gnawed at me, devoured my soul. I would be defined only by my dealings with the protagonist and if that were Bernard, then I would have to do something really meaningful and let him out into the world to change it.

"He's developing Objectivity."

"It happens." The Reverend shrugged, confused that I was still in his office.

"What if it goes further?"

"That would be something. Deep Objectivity is incredibly rare. Almost never happens. There's no way it could be him then. Considering Bernard's inoculations and Sagramore's experiments and whatnot... well, if he develops Deep Objectivity, then there are possibilities. A person with Deep Objectivity and such a high Maya tolerance... but, there's no way he could develop Deep Objectivity. It's a complicated, silly and trite condition."

The Reverend's trembling hands showed me his resolve was not impenetrable. He almost burned himself lighting the cigarette he must have needed to calm his nerves. The thought that I was onto something frazzled him. The realization was too much of a threat to the things he believed, too much of a threat to Authorial Intent at large. He was thinking, but he didn't want to be thinking. It's always seemed to me that if a guy's got faith, he shouldn't have to think so much. Maybe this guy didn't have much faith for a Reverend or maybe his Protagonist was too much of an ideal. He wanted a man to topple the towers of the law, a violent, epic superhero type, not a basement baby whose greatest accolade would be drifting out of selfhood.

"Garrett Cook hasn't written him out of that cell you know," the Reverend's voice wagged a finger at me on the surface, but I knew it for more of a childish taunt than an arch theological argument.

"What if Garrett Cook can't write him out of there?"

The Reverend almost burned himself yet again. I had asked the exact wrong question and I knew it. But, every author had unfinished novels, stories they couldn't tell. If this world was one of them, then life would be outright meaningless, especially for a man like the Reverend John Calvin Jenkins. Plot would *not* preserve, no matter how hard we tried to move with it or to inspire.

"Don't talk like that."

I walked out on the Reverend John Calvin Jenkins and Authorial Intent. I went home and I burnt the pamphlets and the manuscript fragments of this Garrett Cook who would not write my world ahead. Something more than this was necessary. Something drastic. Sneaking into my father's study, I looked up everything I could regarding the mud. My eyes lit up when I realized how I could make Bernard's strange ascension happen.

My father happily obliged when I offered to give Bernard his injections. He being poorly drawn and not particularly bright assumed this must have meant that I had gotten all of this ridiculous protagonist business out of my head and that would be better for everyone. I winked at Bernard as I plunged the syringe, mixed with ordinary tap water, into his arm. His eyes widened and his mouth gaped. A less enlightened individual might have thought his soul was trying to escape. A less enlightened individual might actually be right on this count.

"Clyde?" asked the dresser.

"Clyde?" asked Bernard.

"Clyde?" asked the pillows.

"Clyde?" asked the sheets.

"Clyde?" asked the plexiglass.

"Clyde?" asked my right shoe.

"Clyde?" asked Bernard.

And then Bernard was gone. I had done my work.

I traded the Henderson orangs a crate of bananas for two high caliber handguns, a sniper rifle, ten hand grenades, a gas mask and a shotgun. Though a monkey could fire a gun, they certainly had no notion of the retail value of one. It was all set, I just had to fend off my father, Sagramore and their attack dinosaurs, get Bernard (after figuring out who or what he was) out of there and let my neglected brother reach his destiny. Jealousy and contempt still raged in me, but I had acknowledged my brother's place in the world, while nobody else had. That must count for something, right? It doesn't. Didn't.

Boils my fucking blood to this day.

III

Bernard had been Objective for four days before he saw Archelon Ranch and his longing for freedom, once just an aching emptiness, was now an incendiary passion. He hadn't thought too much of freedom as a possibility before he became the rhamphorhyncus, longed for it more when he became a hat and now would die for it but he still didn't know how to get it. In the morning, his taunting asshole brother, who had devoted his life to selling raptor poison and tormenting him, would come and give him a second, secret injection. The tests and proddings of his father were bad enough and now his brother compounded their sadism. It made him want out even worse. He wanted to tear the house to shreds and do the same to everyone in it. If he could learn to control and focus his fits of Objectivity, maybe he could do it.

But there was no controlling the Objectivity. Over the past day, it had become paradoxically more frequent and more difficult to manage the more he thought of freedom. He tried to fly out of the city as a pterosaur, but his wings were shot off by a rooftop sniper looking for some lunch and he was caught.

He was half alive, but not far from the dust tunnel as the sniper and his wife began to cut him up and serve him. When Bernard came back from this misadventure, he vowed to stop eating meat, which surprised his father, but not Professor Sagramore.

"Objectives get very fussy about their fellow creatures. Very sensitive. "

Bernard was getting a good deal more than "very sensitive". The thoughts and imperatives of his fellow beings grew louder around him each time he went Objective. He had to be extremely careful, since he understood that complete Objectivity would prove worst than fatal. Total Objectivity was like befriending every snowflake in a blizzard and making sure you didn't forget any of their birthdays. Total Objectivity was the worst kind of unbeing, which made him grateful for the security of the basement in the past, maybe now a bit grateful that he wasn't a pterosaur being gutted and stuffed for dinner, or the knife that had to bathe in the guts or the cutting board whose sole purpose was to lie back as food was lain out, soaking with bacteria. Best not to think about the things he was glad he wasn't, as they were quite numerous. The person part of Bernard was beginning to hate the basement and could think of many things that he would rather be, so was developing a better relationship with Objectivity, in spite of the all consuming threat of omnipresence. He was prevented from thinking of these things by an unfortunate three minutes as a margarita and then some time as a fire hydrant.

When he returned from his distraction, his father and Sagramore were standing over him. It was a common sight when coming back from Objectivity, but it was nonetheless an unpleasant one.

"Dear me," said Sagramore, his voice full of concern, "this is no good at all. If he just had Objectivity, it would be fine. He would be just what we're looking for, but now…"

"Do we kill him?" Bernard's father asked, loading a syringe with something unfamiliar. Bernard wished that when this time came, there would be some sign of misery or lament on his father's face, some indication that his son would be a loss. Bernard wished his father felt something and beyond that, that he would be able to feel the something his father felt. Bernard had never missed affection before his Objectivity advanced, but felt the affection the thirsty young woman had for the margarita and was curious about it. It was not love of course, but it was more than the monkey's fondness for the hat, which had been just about the most affection he'd encountered before. There must only be love at Archelon Ranch. There must be love. The golden haired young ladies smiled in his memory, smiles of devotion, tenderness and hope. Bernard was grateful to find that Sagramore was thinking over the proposition instead of giving it an immediate yes. If he died as the Bernard that was Bernard and not one of his adopted selves, he was fairly certain that the dust tunnel would not spit him out as it usually did and his dreams of Archelon Ranch would therefore go unrealized.

"No," said Sagramore, "I don't think that will be necessary. We just need to find the means to anchor him here and then find out exactly what the mud does to an individual genetically programmed to resist it. I think after that, I should be able to make him a Consensual."

"I suppose that's good enough. You must understand, I'm not eager to kill my son."

"Of course not. Who would be?"

"I love my son."

"Of course you do. He is your son."

Bernard was quite certain his father was lying. He was also quite certain that he did not approve of this plan to fix him in consensual reality. If he stayed consensual, he would be stuck in bed until he finally lost it and ended up enduring the visions

Suburbanites had to deal with. He did not want to be a Suburbanite and wasn't sure why he wasn't one already on account of the mud and CRAMPS (Consensual Reality Affirmation Mediator for Permanent Schizmatics). Far as he could tell, it was something in his DNA, something in his mind, something special. He had never considered himself special, but he had to be. He was enduring the mud, after all, and Archelon Ranch had chosen to reach out to him. He would never get there if he couldn't…

I am the dresser drawer. I am full of clothes and I am made of wood. I am a dresser drawer. I am a dresser drawer. I am a dresser drawer and I am a dresser drawer. He reached out in the language of dresser drawers and pleaded his authenticity. He thought of the first time, how strange it was to be stiff and trapped in the dresser and he welcomed it. He closed his eyes and focused on how all beings were not altogether unlike a dresser drawer, especially himself. He had been a dresser once and he would be it again. I am a dresser drawer I am a dresser drawer I am a dresser drawer I am a dresser drawer hello dresser drawer I am a dresser hello to you dresser drawer I am a dresser drawer I am also Bernard I am a dresser drawer what are you talking about I am a sheet I am a sheet hello sheet I am a bed I am the plexiglass I am Bernard I am I am I am I am I am…

He faded from the bed and was once more something else. He was big, he was hungry, he stomped through town picking up pedestrians with his mouth gnashing them into a fine paste. His biggest, most prominent, thought was "I am hungry". He was not sure what made him hungry or what made his distaste for meat disappear completely, but this Bernard, the tyrannosaurus rex Bernard, wanted to eat people. The message was still there for him, perhaps ready in the mind of every tyrannosaurus rex. Something had prepared this self for him, the one thing he needed most to know. Archelon Ranch is beyond the city, Archelon Ranch touches the eternal sea, the sea of seas that cannot be corrupted, the sea outside of time. Love and delight and devotion wait for you. They wait for you past the gates of Archelon Ranch. If there is just one place to go, choose Archelon Ranch. Archelon Ranch is calling and it waits for you. He reached out past this self and sought to take his flight. He reached for the place, for unity with the marble, the sea or the great sea turtles. He sought nothing more than to be one of those turtles, but the turtles said, "You are not, you are not a turtle and you are not. You cannot cheat. There are no short-cuts to Archelon Ranch. There is one road only."

He cried gigantic dinosaur tears as he felt the place from which hope and love must have originated reject him. He stomped and ate and cried and contemplated what had to be done. Bernard reached for the Bernard part of him and saw the bed and cell and syringes, the wicked father and the crass, hateful brother. He stomped through the city knowing what would have to be done. As the body tugged away, he tugged back, affirmed Bernard and the tyrannosaurus to be one and the same. The DPW triceratops hurled itself at him, but he had strength, passion, jaws of steel and a desperate need for love to protect him. Police and triceratopses and angry gang members could do nothing to stand against him. Home. Hope. Love. Archelon Ranch is calling Archelon Ranch is calling.

The house, small, petty and angry thing, stood tall, but not tall enough. He raised his clawed feet and gave it several hard kicks, then buffeted all of his scaled body against it. Pounding with his angry, saurian head, he burst through the wall, looming over his father and a terrified Professor Sagramore. He lifted his colossal legs and brought them down on weak, sadistic humans. Bernard returned to Bernard and found himself wading through wreckage where he found a gun that his father must have kept in case the now dead guard dinosaurs went wild. He walked out of the house, or what was left of it, for what would be the last time (and considering that he was usually sedated and dragged out for his trips to the community pool, sort of the first) and set out for Archelon Ranch.

IV

I watched from the Hendersons' roof as my plan
to make a hero out of Bernard began to come to
fruition. My Deep Objective brother had become a
tyrannosaurus and brought bloody, screaming death
to Sagramore and our father. It's not as if our father
didn't deserve it, or wasn't written for eating, but
I still felt a bit sad, having just been party to what
must have been a particularly agonizing death for
him. I had just allowed my flesh and blood to kill off
my flesh and blood to prove a theory and establish
my own existential relevance but the funny thing
about that was once I stopped feeling kind of sad,
I felt important. I felt big and useful. This stagnant
loop of tropical death we call a city was ready for
change now. All Bernard had to do now was... he
would have to just... he could... and then you know
there was...

Well, fuck. It wasn't THAT far ahead, and yet
somehow I had managed not to plan that far ahead.
At least I had given him a gun, since Garrett Cook's
work tended to be on the violent side and he would
probably have something to shoot. I decided maybe I

should give him some space to get his bearings and we could plan out his heroic future together.

As he emerged from the ruins of our house and picked up the gun, I felt relieved, like things were finally on track after the years of suffering that had fallen upon this city at the hands of the tyrant sadist hack, Garrett Cook and his stagnating plot. How long ago should this turn of events have been written? How long ago should this have started moving forward? How long ago should Bernard have gotten free and initiated his mission of glorious redemption? These questions hounded me, sickened me and gnawed at me. I was starting to really hate Garrett Cook and his damn imagination. I could thank him for life, but I could thank myself more. I had a right to my hate, but it still felt good thinking that I could leave it behind soon enough now that Bernard was free and the protagonist could set the wheels of justice in motion.

I climbed down from the roof but still chose to dart behind things as I stalked my brother, curious what would come next. Not that it was my concern. Now that the narrative was being rectified, I probably had little more to do with it. But I'd still get to enjoy my life a little bit more knowing everything would be okay. Unless Bernard was going to be some kind of martyr; not altogether out of the question. Government cyborgs could end up ripping out his brain and the reader would be left with a sad familiar feeling and a desire to stamp out oppression. That would be no good. Couldn't risk it. I had no idea how audacious it was of me to keep following my brother until his victory was clear.

From my vantage point behind a trash can, I first heard the accursed phrase. Like the words "christmas" or "blowjob", it was a sparkling, ominous fireworks show of language that would explode new priorities into life. "Archelon Ranch" he kept mumbling until he took a deep breath and sat down on the curb to think. Archelon Ranch. It sounded beautiful.

It sounded dangerous. Some great conspiracy, some colossal secret that only a person who had attained forbidden unity with the All could hear about. I kept the volume of my cellphone and voice low as I called the man who, sadly enough, was the only one who would know what Archelon Ranch was. I had thought I had parted company with Authorial Intent forever, but there was nobody else I could think of calling.

"Hello?" said the Reverend Calvin Jenkins.

"This is Clyde."

"Give me one reason I shouldn't hang up on you, you rotten son-of-a-bitch..."

"Bernard is free and he has Deep Objectivity."

"That's vaguely interesting."

"What is Archelon Ranch?"

The line went dead for long enough that I suspected he would make good his threat to hang up. There was heavy breathing on the other end, real heavy, the sound of a man who needed a paper bag to hyperventilate into. Now I knew this phrase had power. Now I knew it had meaning and that it was loaded with sinister purpose.

"Reverend?"

"Plot be preserved. Where did you hear that?"

I turned up the phone's volume and pointed it towards my brother, who had resumed his awestruck, confused mumbling. His time deliberating was no respite from his renewed obsession.

"Archelon Ranch, Archelon Ranch..."

I quickly turned the phone down again before Bernard could hear the voice on the other end. I didn't want him to know that I was out there. In his addled state he would no doubt remember me as the guy who stuck extra syringes in him for leisure instead of as the mastermind who ignored the naysayers and pulled off his risky and highly abstract rescue.

"Your brother is talking about Archelon Ranch?!"

"That's where I heard it."

"Plot preserve..."

I was sure he could feel the thick, glowing superior smirk on my face straight through the phone. There could be no doubts now, no matter how much a shell-shocked space cadet my brother was. He knew about whatever Archelon Ranch was after all. As the door to door Campbellians would say, he had received the call.

"Your brother might be the protagonist, hard as it is for me to accept it. I really expected someone more stable, but I should have realized this whole thing is by Garrett Cook and Garrett Cook doesn't write about stable people. Hindsight is twenty/twenty... but don't take that as a definite acknowledgement. I'm still going to have to run some tests."

"Okay, but what is Archelon Ranch?"

"You could say it's a kind of..."

I was getting impatient. If my brother were less spacy, I would have thought that he was going to leave and I would have to resume my mobile stalking efforts. He had stopped mumbling about Archelon Ranch and was now loudly telling himself that he was not the sidewalk. I was glad that I had read up on Deep Objectivity and knew that over time without contact with the mud, it could be controlled; particularly by a superior mind or a designer human. My brother was a designer human with a superior (though malnourished) mind.

"Archelon Ranch is a very special place."

"Do you know what it is or don't you?"

"There are a number of things. The author's obsessed with the phrase. It's haunted him for some time, but he's never been able to do anything with it."

"It's gibberish? It's nothing?"

The Reverend laughed a remarkable haughty laugh that made me hate him again.

"Oh, no. Quite the opposite. It's THE thing."

"What does that mean?"

"It's the place where the big secret is held. It could be a realm of cowboy mystery or a secret government

36

brainwashing facility or a fucked up postmodern madhouse. The thing is, it could be all of these things, but it's probably none of them. For it to actually figure into the plot, it has to be something wonderful, something wonderful and safe that's more than just a mantra."

"A paradise. He's a prophet leading us on an exodus from this city."

"I'm not saying it's impossible, but I'm still going to need to run some tests."

"Okay, so do it."

"You stay out of it this time. I need to know."

"Okay."

"I mean it!"

"Okay, get on with it, then!"

The thugs parked their motorcycles across the street a minute later. There were five of them. One was huge with an eye patch, one was a lady wielding a chain whip and there were three nearly identical bruisers with shotguns. I recognized all of these guys, and it was easy to predict what was coming.

The huge muscular Narrativist with the eye patch charged at Bernard first and put his weight into it. The kick came just as he did. It was a mighty roundhouse from Bernard that broke several of the guy's ribs. Though Bernard was smaller, he hit ridiculously hard, smashing the Narrativist's jaw off its hinge with a vicious uppercut. The big guy thought of reaching for the knife at his side, but had to stop himself, devout Narrativist that he was. With another quick combination Bernard brought the thug to his knees and then to the ground.

The three thugs with shotguns caulked their weapons but with unnatural speed and grace Bernard outdrew each one of them, gunning them down before even one could fire. Living in this city as long as I have, I had grown used to seeing people die. Every time it happened, it felt ugly and pointless, like it only happened because that's what fucking happened, but with Bernard it was different; every time he killed, it was poetic. When he shot those guys down, it was quick, graceful and down-right sensible. I would have thought that the girl with the whip would have learnt a lesson from her unfortunate companions, but she didn't. She didn't see him holstering the gun as she charged at him, snapping her whip. He grabbed it mid snap, and with the same animal grace with which he'd shot the men with shotguns down. He wrapped it around her neck, squeezing hard. In under ten seconds, all five thugs sent for my brother were dead. I had never seen him wield a gun before and knew we never gave him lessons in martial arts, but he killed like nothing else in nature killed. It didn't take me long to figure out why, either.

Objectivity. He knew when they were coming, how their bodies worked. He could hear the gun explaining how and when to fire. I was beginning to get the author's intent and it was a great relief to see that my brother had been chosen for a good reason. He was the man who was going to bring us where we were going. He was the one who would lead us to Archelon Ranch. Whatever the place was, it had to be special and Bernard would have to be a special and beautiful man to get us there.

My arrogant smirk returned as the large man's cellphone rang idly five, six, seven times. Then mine rang.

"He got them all, Reverend. Quick too. That boy can kill."

"Yes, he's the one."

"And he's going to Archelon Ranch."

"Plot preserve."

"Plot preserve."

I felt far less cheated than I had before. When I first figured it out, I resented the hell out of the author, but now it didn't feel so bad. With a surge of pride and confidence, I approached my brother, hugging him for what had to be the first time he had been hugged by anyone.

"Do you see it now, Bernard? You're the guy! You're the protagonist!"

Bernard's expression was blank. His eyes hung wide open, vast and stupid. There was no recognition behind them. For some reason, I played along. I let go of him as though it was a case of mistaken identity. Could he have been joking? Had Bernard encountered joking somewhere? Had he been a joke?

"You're the protagonist, Bernard!"

He shrugged and walked off, the confused expression traded for one of sharp, focused zen intensity. My heart sank and I felt once again like I was a bit part, once more as if I hadn't been written, once more as if the effort it took to assert my being was all for nothing. Bernard was not thanking me for all my efforts. Bernard was not going to heal society or make the world safe for me again. This was not my book. This book did not belong to the city or the Narrativists.

"Take us with you!" I screamed, "Take us with you! This place is Hell! Take me with you!"

The *us* of course became me because I was more concerned for myself than anything. It didn't make me a hypocrite. Bernard was the hero. The man for whom this book had been written and he didn't even know me, didn't even know his own brother. Awful though our relationship was, I was his brother and I had helped him. Made me wonder what the point of life was and if Bernard was its star — the center of it all. I could come up with very little to think about but the repeated awful realization that he was not taking me or anybody else with him, that this was his quest. I looked around me at the hot, vine covered rainforest city and my feelings toward Garrett Cook shifted into hate again. I hated Garrett Cook more than anything, though my world was too small to have much hatred in it. If he would have paradise, I would have it too. I would make it my own. Hell, I'd do everything in my power to make sure that at the end, it was me at the Archelon Ranch, not that selfish little shit, Bernard.

V

Bernard was now free. Free and alone in a world that he knew only through the experiences of other entities. He knew only where he longed to go and that it lay outside the city. There had to be some way he could figure all this out, some way to know. He sat on the curb and witnessed the carnage of Cooling Time. As the citizens emerged to risk death to beat the heat, he found himself affirming that he wanted very much to never see this terrible place again. As he knew of but two places, the city and Archelon Ranch, he decided that to get to Archelon Ranch, all he really needed to do was get out of the city and the only way he knew of to get out of the city was through the Mall. At the East, there was the Mall, at the Westernmost edge of the city, there was the Mall, to the North and to the South in a great ring of plastic and neon circling the city there was the Mall.

He reached out for the message and for the image of Archelon Ranch and it came, the same bright message, the same peerless sky and marble temple. He begged one of the turtles to tell him the way, but there was no response. It smiled its wise, ancient turtle smile and looked off into the distance at a beautiful future, devoid of sweat and death, a future this city didn't deserve.

"Tell me, tell me..."

There was only quiet wisdom, only cosmic superiority. Only the knowledge that outside the city lay Archelon Ranch. He didn't even know which of the four entrances of the Mall to take to exit the city. Knowing nothing of the world, he had to trust his instincts, instincts that said west. So, the only thing he could do, the only logical thing, was to go west. If he had money, he could have taken the subway, but the subway was pretty much nothing but a nest for the colossal spiders that crawled through the sewers hoping hapless people and beasts would fall into their gaping, fanged mouths. A cab would be better, but very few cabs ran in the city and they were costly. He closed his eyes, begging his body to become Objective, telling it he was a pterosaur or an airplane (though those were far rarer than pterosaurs, considering the difficulties native to navigating a sky canopy). I am a chimpanzee I am a pterosaur I am I am I am I am starving. He had just eaten — no, the tyrannosaur had just eaten. His body was a pinnacle of neglect. The turtle had said no cheating, so perhaps only Bernard could be the Bernard at Archelon Ranch. Bernard the Bernard. The Bernard that barely existed. Bernard the starving, Bernard the disoriented.

In his state of disorientation and hunger, Bernard ended up simply wandering west, whilst his feet grew more tired and his body more hungry. His body did not have the energy to simply wander west toward a mall that might not be there with no food in its neglected stomach, so he collapsed on the street. As he went down, he tried to think of all the creatures that had it so much worse than he did, but all of those creatures had to eat too, so these thoughts were shot down where they stood. I am Bernard the Bernard the probably dying from years of injections and only rare instances of exercise at the community pool.

Hope caught up to starvation in the form of a young woman about eighteen in a mint green bikini. Her hair was dyed the same color. Her body was lean and her face cute, warm and pleasant.

"You poor man!" she exclaimed, "You look about ready to pass out on the pavement! Are you hungry?"

In spite of having *been* many strangers, Bernard was not used to speaking to them as himself. It took him some time to figure out what to say.

"Yes, I'm very hungry. Do you know where food is?"

"Yeah. Come on. I'll get you something." She beckoned him into a convenient little corner restaurant. Bernard had never been in a restaurant before.

The girl led Bernard up to the counter, where a middle aged Italian lady clad in a short silk kimono was cleaning up and taking orders.

"Hi there!" said the lady, who was dark, voluptuous and not careworn in the least.

"Hi."

"What can I get you?" she asked.

He knew of several foods he had eaten but very few that he specifically liked. His father usually tended to make a flat, synthetic meat with refried beans for protein and instant cornbread for carbohydrates, foods put together with no intention but to keep a test subject strong enough for testing. He had a favorite cereal, but could not remember the name of it, which was a shame because he didn't really have a favorite anything else, besides a preference for reading White Fang in his DNA instead of Call of the Wild.

"I don't really know. What's good?"

It was a general question, not "what's good here?" but rather "what things that people eat are good to eat?"

The Italian lady touched his arm and smiled.

"Rigatoni with meatballs and a nice, frosty glass of Shifatsu Superfun Carbobev. Sound good to you?"

He'd had Carbobev before and he liked the taste. It gave him a nice boost for the day. He was not too certain what rigatoni or meatballs were, but they didn't sound like they were all that bad.

"I don't know what rigatoni is, but I'm sure it's good. "

"It is," said the mint green girl, "Cindy's a great cook."

"Then I look forward to it." Bernard smiled. He was lucky professor Sagramore brushed his teeth thoroughly with Mega-wyt three times a day and twice in the evening. Bernard's teeth, unlike the rest of him were pristine and shiny.

The mint green girl smiled back.

"You've got a really nice smile."

"So do you."

The mint green girl sipped her Sparkling Bog-peach carbobev with feigned shyness. Cindy had given Bernard 20th Century Retro flavor which was syrupy and brown but was still good. He could not think of any flavor he had encountered which was as good as 20th Century Retro. There was no pretense of imitation, no attempt to mask its inorganic nature. It was strangely original.

"Does it come in Synthberry?" he asked Cindy, who responded by pouring him a glass of Synthberry Carbobev. Bernard switched back and forth between sips of the two flavors and the result was sweet, potent and invigorating. He could feel his usually numb body springing to life, being something more than just a rickety cage for a powerful mind and soul. Carbobev was made with trace amounts of Supra-Adderall 7, which reacted intensely to the chemicals in artificial synthberry flavor. He was not used to these effects, since the Supra-Adderall 7 was carefully portioned in breakfast cereals, as breakfast cereals were now solely given to very small children and experimental test subjects. In Carbobev, it was used with wild abandon. Bernard had known nothing of restaurants outside of the time he had spent as a martini. He had not been too sure about them back then, but was now certain they were pretty great. He hoped that the rest of his journey would be so leisurely, but he knew from his experiences as various other creatures that it could not be, especially since he had heard ghastly things about the Mall from his brother's breakfast conversation.

"What's the matter?" the mint green girl asked.

Cindy touched his shoulder.

"You okay?"

The mint green girl reached into the crotch of her bikini and pulled out four Naders and a Sarandon and gave it to him. It was a lot of money, particularly to get from a total stranger. He had spent little time as people during his Objectivity, so had only the proddings of his father, his brother and Professor Sagramore and the whining, incontinent children at the community pool to judge mankind by. He knew his fellow men as creatures who thoughtlessly devoured innocent martinis and skinned majestic pterosaurs for food. No solid impressions, hunters and victims like the rest of nature, but no signs of a benevolent streak in them, no deeply redeeming qualities. But in the mint green girl's act of generosity he saw something he had never seen before. He felt like crying. Bernard hadn't thought to cry in most situations. He had learned from a very young age, that for a test subject like him, crying did little good and would grant no clemency. It was a violation of protocol and not right for one of his station. He did not cry. He sat there numb and silent, knowing no suitable reply. Could there be other people like this?

"Thank you," he stammered, "that's what people say, isn't it?"

The mint green girl couldn't help but laugh.

GARRETT COOK

"Yes, thank you is what people say when they get a gift."

"Good."

Cindy brought out the plate of rigatoni. Bernard was fascinated. It was hot, red and shaped like little tubes. There were huge, crimson chunks of meat on top of it. He no longer felt the revulsion toward eating the flesh of animals that he had picked up during his time as the pterosaur. He was a ravenous predator and the plate of pasta delivered on all of its primal promises.

He had never seen so much food before (beyond of course an entire pterosaur). This big round plate of goodness reminded him of his time as a tyrannosaurus, which a dark, perverse part of him treasured. Almost made him regret that he never bothered to eat anyone during that time.

"Is it good?" Cindy asked.

"Thank you," he said. He spat out tiny chunks of meatball as he did so.

"You're welcome, sweetie."

"So, where are you going exactly?" the mint green girl inquired.

"The Mall."

A man at a nearby table stood up and sat down next to Bernard. He was quite overdressed for this heat, wearing a tank-top and long shorts made of a thick, coarse blue material. His hair was white and his body rotund. He extended his hand and Bernard shook it.

"Chuck Callaway."

"Bernard."

"Did I hear you're goin' to the Mall?"

"Yeah, in fact I am."

Chuck pulled a deck of cards out of his pocket and fanned it out.

"Pick a card."

Bernard drew the Ace of Chainsaws.

"Now put it back."

Bernard complied and Chuck Callaway shuffled the cards. He smiled as he pulled out the Ace of Chainsaws. Bernard wondered if this man had become Objective and asked the deck of cards where the Ace was.

"Well, Bernard, is this your card… hell, that rhymes don't it? Is this your card, Bernard?"

"Yes, yes it is."

"That's a stitch, huh?"

"Yeah."

"Learned that one from when I lived with the comprachicos. Those bastards kept me three years before my folks found me again and bought me back, but I don't really hold no grudge. Taught me how to be tough and clever. Taught me how to wrestle a compsognathus blindfolded. People talk a lot of shit about comprachicos but they're not so bad once you get to know 'em. You know any comprachicos, son?"

Bernard shook his head.

"You're a shy one, aintcha? You know what they say about the shy ones, don'tcha? Comprachicos used to say a shy fella will steal your sister and fuck your wallet and when he's done, you get 'em both back fulla spooge."

Cindy laughed a high, nasal pleasant laugh.

"Old Chuck's a rascal, but don't pay him no mind. He's a bit like them comprachicos he was talkin' about; he might look like a criminal, but once you get to know him, he is a fine, stand-up human bein' who's just a little short on social graces and manners."

Chuck gave Cindy a mock bow.

"I apologize if I offend milady. Outside, I have parked my chariot, which can take yonder gentleman to the Mall if he doth wish it so and desires the pleasure of my company."

It did not occur to Bernard to laugh.

"Thank you. I could definitely use a ride."

Bernard finished his lunch, while Chuck grabbed a ham and pterosaur sandwich to go. Together, they stepped into Chuck's red pickup. As he got into the passenger seat, Bernard closed his eyes, not wishing to witness all the squalor around him or any of the city's numerous tableaus of suffering. He wanted instead to dream of Archelon Ranch's splendors and reflect upon the kindness of people like Chuck and Cindy and the mint green girl. For all of the avuncular pretenses, Chuck seemed to understand a lot. He made no conversation.

It's too hot. The thought struck Bernard from nowhere, a bullet from a sniper inside his head. It's too hot. We're going to die we're going to die we're going to die. When will they turn the fans on again? I hope they like my new hat. When will they turn the fans on again? Chop chop chop. Meat, I smell meat. Shut up. I am Bernard. I am Bernard. I am a truck you are a truck. I am the sidewalk you are the sidewalk I am Bernard I am a truck what did you say I am Bernard I am a truck make up your mind. I am a truck you are a truck otherwise we couldn't talk. When will they turn the fans on again? I am a truck I am not a truck. With food in his belly and his body starting to recover, the Objectivity's drives were returning and it would not take no for an answer. We're all going to die you know we're all going to die when will the fans come on when will the damn fans come on I am a fan I am a fan help them I am a fan when will the fans come on I am a truck make up your I am a truck I am a fan I am a truck you are a truck I am a truck make up your mind I am a fan I am a truck when will the fans come on dammit meat, I smell meat chop chop I am a sidewalk hello calm down kid what the hell's wrong with you you're starting to freak me out. As he realized he was becoming Chuck he began to panic and could almost not feel himself. He concentrated on Archelon Ranch, looked ahead into the turtles, knowing they were the only beings that would push him away. You are not a sea turtle you are not a sea turtle there is no cheating.

He breathed deeply, focused on his body and tried to become once more certain that he was Bernard. This was a difficult thing to convince himself of. Two days ago, it would have been impossible. He meditated on the soft and battered seats and began to understand the sensation of sitting on them. Moment by moment, he got closer to the sensation of wanting to be Bernard until at last he had done it; he had successfully controlled an Objective fit, which would no doubt be helpful further in on his journey. Becoming every blade of grass would certainly not do him much good on his quest, since blades of grass don't even have legs. Painful as it was, Bernard opened his eyes and looked upon the city's West Side, which was always chaotic, as if choked by perpetual Cooling Time crowds.

There was an epidemic of homelessness on the West Side. Ragged, naked twitching people clutched at homemade spears for dear life. Others struggled for survival by poking local jaguars with flaming sticks, a weapon far less effective on deinonychi and gilawalruses that jumped up from the sewers to find food. A wiry twelve year old boy put up an admirable fight against one of the striped, scaly pinipeds which had begun gnawing on his baby sister. The boy aimed an improvised shortbow at it. He would have hit his target, but did not see the mosquito flying overhead. It was a small one, only the size of a large dog, but it made up for its stature with tenacity, shoving its proboscis four inches deep into the kid's flesh. His healthy, surprisingly tan skin actually grew several shades whiter as the bug exsanguinated him completely, as mosquitoes tended to do.

"That, my friend is why I voted for the arm the homeless initiative," said Chuck. They were the first words he'd spoken since they got into the car.

"It's horrible," Bernard replied.

But, the boy didn't die in vain. The gilawalrus spat out the boy's baby sister and shimmied up the lamppost after one of its favorite foods, now even juicier since it was bloated with fresh blood. Most people who did not live on the West Side did not know that gilawalruses climbed, Bernard included. The movement of the creature's dextrous fins was quite surprising. Before the mosquito could take off, one of the gilawalrus' sharp tusks punctured its large but fragile right wing and dragged it down to the lamppost and into the sewer.

"Nature sure is funny, ain't it?"

"Yeah."

They passed three similar scenes. Gilawalrus infestation had become a big problem, one that the government swore they would address once they resolved the security issue in the suburbs. It was possible that gilawalruses were meant to be that very solution as they had, after all, put a good deal of money into documenting and augmenting the infestation, as well as linking gilawalrus tunnels to the Mall so that Suburbanites could not get into the city through there. Professor Sagramore and Bernard's father debated the gilawalrus situation often and they tended to decide that the government was making the wrong choice.

When they passed the West Side, Bernard was deeply relieved and very grateful for Chuck Callaway and his truck (trucks being one of only three things gilawalruses did not attack, the other two being tyrannosaurs and the deadly Standardizers) but did not much like the look of the crowd outside the Mall. Between the toothless comprachicos and the men selling domesticated raptors and jaguars, it looked bad. The fat, the deformed, the old and the naked came together in what looked like a rally for fat elderly deformed naked rights. There were no healthy, no decent people heading into the Mall. As he sat in line behind a pair of Suburbanites and a stage magician, with a gilawalrus in a gigantic cat carrier that he dragged inches behind him on a chain, he was getting an idea of what obstacles lay between him and the bliss of Archelon Ranch.

VI

I am not a soldier. I am not a burglar. I am not a ninja. So, my brother managed to lose me in the Cooling Time crowd. By the time I found him, he was running off with a girl with green hair who I recognized from the Narrativist lecture and had been thinking of asking out. My chances of being able to do that were probably somewhat narrow now and if he did walk away with some chick from the Narrativist church, I would have no fucking chance at all of catching up to him. I decided to use my natural aptitudes to my advantage instead of having to rely upon skills I didn't have. I was sneaky, not stealthy but sneaky. Sneaky enough to get away with giving Bernard extra injections without anybody suspecting a thing. I figured I would use that sneakiness to execute a clever gambit that ended in catching my brother and forcing him at gunpoint to take me to Archelon Ranch. This plan did not incorporate the evidence I had previously acquired regarding my brother's skills as a ruthless, unstoppable fighting machine, but otherwise, it sounded absolutely fucking brilliant. It began with a phone call.

"Hello, Reverend. Plot preserve."

"Plot preserve, Clyde."

"I'm calling to ask you a very important question."

"Ask away. After what you've done for us, I owe you one."

"Where is my brother?"

Silence. Laughter. He hung up then called me right back.

"Are you kidding me?"

"What?"

"Are you fucking kidding me, Clyde? You have got to be fucking kidding me. That is the sort of question that only somebody who is fucking kidding me would ask. That's pretty damn stupid, Clyde."

I growled.

I breathed heavy.

"Why Reverend is that the sort of question somebody who is fucking kidding you would ask? I'm calling you to find out the whereabouts of my brother. It's not unusual for a guy to ask where his brother is, is it? I don't think it's a very difficult question either. I haven't lost track of him for very long and I certainly doubt that you have, Reverend."

Patronizing laughter on the other end again. I wouldn't have taken this shit yesterday. I had to right now, because any sign of hostility would betray my intentions. I waited until the laughter stopped. It was killing me, but I let him keep laughing, keep reminding me that I was nobody relevant, that I almost wasn't even part of this story. But I was about to prove to him just how important I was.

"No. There's your answer, Clyde. No. In fact, I'm going to say fuck no. I'm not going to do that for you."

"And why not, Reverend?"

"First of all, I myself don't even know."

"That's bullshit, Reverend. I don't believe it for a second."

"Don't take that tone with me, Clyde."

"I'm sorry. I found Bernard for you, didn't I?"

"Yes, you did, Clyde, plot preserve, and I and all Narrativists are extremely thankful to you..." I bit my tongue and waited for whatever gigantic bullshit bus of a "sorry, no dice" phrase was coming up. In my head I already heard a painfully patronizing BUT. What came out the Reverend's mouth next was not a BUT, which was pretty diplomatic for a guy like him. Instead, I got a stern, very bad news, HOWEVER.

"HOWEVER, this is extremely important fate-of-all-existence business that I refuse to treat lightly. I can think of no business more relevant. We simply cannot afford to treat this lightly and give out information like that, even to you, his brother. I'd be letting down my parish, I'd be letting down Bernard and letting down existence itself, which you must remember, Clyde, you happen to be a part of. I'd be letting *you* down if I told you or anyone. I simply can't do it. I've told my operatives to take him wherever he needs to go and not to tell me where. You know, Clyde, in case something occurs."

"I'm afraid I don't follow, Reverend. What the hell kind of something could occur that should make it impossible for the head of the Narrativist church and Bernard's own brother to know his whereabouts?"

"All kinds of things. Your brother's a runaway test subject who will determine the fate of existence and prove that Narrativist doctrine is the true faith. There can be kidnapping, torture, brainwashing, bribery, temporary insanity. People say things sometimes under duress. I don't want to be one of those people. I can't compromise Bernard for anything or anyone."

"But, I'm his brother!" I wasn't too happy about it, but I couldn't help bringing it up.

"I know you are, Clyde, and you should be proud. You should be thinking about the great things you're doing for society."

Wandering the pyramid of this conversation, I tripped off a pressure plate, that fired out little darts of inspiration. I could see my way around this plan and had found the angle I needed. It was a damn good angle, too. I smiled inwardly at my guile, although it was actually some of the Reverend's earlier words that had given me the idea.

"Could we talk in private?"

"I suppose we could. You appear to be having a crisis of faith and it is my duty to deal with crises of faith in my parishioners."

"I appreciate it."

Retaining sincerity and refusing to explode and riddle the Reverend with shrapnel of arrogant laughter was difficult. I didn't believe in him anymore, so it was easy to lie, but it was hard to act like I had respect for this guy. It was approaching impossible in fact. The faith was a joke. The book was a joke. Its author was a joke who had only had one book published that sold few enough copies you could count 'em on your digits. I myself, though clever enough to wrangle my way into the narrative without the author's permission was already a sick joke. It was as hard not to laugh as it was not to cry. I had to act as if I knew none of these things, which were now intrinsic to who I was.

"I'll be free after my lecture on choreographing incidental debauchery. It's pretty important if we're in something by Garrett Cook. Shall we meet in my office or is there somewhere else you'd prefer?"

"Your office is perfect." Easy. Shooting fish in a barrel. Trading drugs to monkeys.

The hour was more than enough time for me to convince my boss I wanted to pick up another shift and do a run today. This was a crucial part of my plan. I needed the van to load up the supplies the orangs were taking care of for me. Luckily for me, I had anticipated that my brother would leave nothing of the house behind. In my infinite cleverness, I had also saved up some emergency shoots, leaves and grubs that could be traded for chloroform and rope. With these things stashed in the van, I drove to the meeting, stashing a gun in the pocket of my white, cotton robe.

When I came into his office, we were friends. He jumped up from his desk and embraced me.

"Plot preserve, Reverend!"

"Plot preserve, Clyde."

I drew the gun and pointed it at his head.

"This is about Bernard, isn't it?" he asked, trembling.

"No."

Though his office had been freonlocked to 55 degrees, the Reverend was sweating bullets. If he made any sudden movements he'd have to deal with one more.

"What is this about, then?"

"This is about Archelon Ranch."

"I told you, I don't know what it is."

"Hand me your cellphone."

He complied and I pocketed it. I kicked the laptop on his desk closed. He had to have had an autodial program on it. Optimist or not, believer in the greater good or not, the Reverend was extremely paranoid and he wore it like a neon orange top hat. He threw up his arms in resignation and I led him out the back door and into my van, where I tied his hands. He was polite and quiet for a couple minutes until he came out with exactly what I expected to hear."

"I don't know where to find your brother, I told you."

"But your operatives do, Reverend."

"I could give them a call if you'd like."

I mulled over it before I caught onto his game. He dials the number; the operatives come looking for him because he has to have been kidnapped. In fact, he's probably told them already not to make any contact or look for him, because they, as the current custodians of the Protagonist were far more important than he. It was a good move and a clever one, but it wouldn't work on me.

"Nice try, Reverend, but I'm not that stupid. I ought to shoot you for that."

"Go ahead."

I shook my head. There were things I was beginning to understand about this man, things about Narrativism that were in his blood. If I was a bad man for selling children raptor spray or having my father killed by a tyrannosaurus rex, I was a worse man for thinking what I was now thinking. It was sick. It was as sick as the cosmic joke we all lived in, sick as the repulsive, unfair plot of the book that made selfish, flaky Bernard into the hero. I shudder to say what I told him because it was the worst way of turning a man's heart against itself.

"You can't die. You have to know the ending. If I kill you, you'll never discover what happens, so like it or not, you have to comply with my demands or else you'll never know what Bernard was meant to do and you'll never know if he reached Archelon Ranch and you'll never know just what he found there if he did."

The Reverend's face became that of a child who had just seen his puppy run over by his own father. Nowadays, puppies are pretty rare, so it's a truly awful look to have on your face and I'm a truly awful man for having put it there. It changed into an "I'm going to tear out your eyes and ejaculate into the sockets" look, which I liked better then shifted back to the puppy one again.

"But you want to stop him," he argued.

What I said next was just as bad, just as exploitative and just as much a product of my jealousy and malice. Boy it was clever and boy it was shitty.

"But, if Bernard's the Protagonist and I'm nobody, I can't stop him. Nobody can stop him and if they do it's what the narrative wants. So, what's the problem? You can't do anything to stop the narrative, can you Reverend? Or is everything you tell yourself and everything you preach for everybody's good all lies? You don't think you're a liar, do you Reverend?"

Now he felt as annoyed as I had been on the telephone with him. He was the one choking back all that bile. It felt now like we were just about even and I was actually doing something to him that hurt him as much as he'd hurt me. He was trapped and he knew it. I don't think I'd ever known two people to be as sickened by each other as we were at that moment.

"No, I'm not a liar and there's nothing you can do to shake my faith. Nothing."

"The last thing I want to do is shake your faith. It's all you've got right now."

No, I didn't want to shake it. I wanted to exploit it, poison it, send it through a hamster maze of paradoxes, but I didn't want to shake it. His faith could take me to Archelon Ranch where I would live peacefully while my brother rotted in the ground, punished for his selfishness. His faith would prove my existential import, which would more than make up for what it had done to me before.

"You shouldn't go through with this," he warned me, "there can be serious repercussions."

I slapped him. I slapped him real hard too. Then I slapped him again. It was hard to get myself to stop, but I had better ways to get revenge. I could do far worse things to this man than slap him.

"Why? It doesn't matter what I do, remember? I'm a nobody, Reverend. If you try to stop me, you only succeed in proving that I'm a threat to the Protagonist. You can't do it."

"You might be the Antagonist."

I played with the idea. That would be something. Being a man who could destroy Bernard's world completely, an agent of the old world order, a monster born of jungle chaos, letting it loose everywhere I go. Bullshit. No, the Antagonist was someone or something far more exotic. Garrett Cook wouldn't allow a guy like me even *that* privilege. He didn't have much respect for people like me. Besides, if I were the Antagonist, I wouldn't have to Assert myself so hard

GARRETT COOK

to exist in the first place. I'd be a bigger, more functional part of the story. I would be fully developed. I would have a hookhand or an army of supernatural entities at my beck and call. What really tipped me off was the burst of snarky laughter that overcame the Reverend. He was absolutely eating all of this up. He'd found a chink in my armor, just as fast as I'd found one in his. I shut him up with a punch in the stomach.

"Fuck you!" I screamed.

"Fuck you!" I punched him again.

"Fuck! Fuck! Fuck!" I couldn't stop. As before he had offered me a taste of relevance and then taken it from me before I could truly partake of it. I was still stupid enough to trust him a bit, cynical though I might have been. This guy was poison — much more venomous and dangerous than I could be. Just as I had trapped him in this paradox, so too had he trapped me. We were each other's prisoners. If I was right about the things that trapped him in his state, he was right too, and if I was wrong, we were wrong together. Did I believe I could change the plot? Did I really believe I could bring down Bernard? The argument was too exhausting; it ensnared us.

"Where can I go?"

"Nowhere."

I should have started punching again, but it would numb him to the pain, lessen the significance of the violence. I waited and let him remember that his life was in my hands whether he liked it or not and that every uncooperative action he took was another step closer to death and ignorance of Bernard's future and the purpose of the book.

"North. I know of a place."

"You had better not be fucking with me, you know that?"

"I know that, Clyde. I know it very well and I promise I'm not fucking with you. Beyond the suburbs to the North is the Sad House. If we get to the Sad House, we can find some answers."

"What's there?"

I hoped that wasn't one of those things like Archelon Ranch that he actually knew nothing about. Archelon Ranch sounded wonderful and I can take wonderful surprises, but the Sad House sounded miserable and I couldn't take miserable surprises very well. I also didn't like that the only possibility lay in another piece of Narrativist mythology. Maybe Narrativist mythology often had a certain chilling accuracy, but it was still something I didn't like depending on. Maybe he knew so little that shooting him and going with my instincts the rest of the way wouldn't be such a bad idea. It couldn't turn out any worse than having to live with him. Hmm... shoot him or indulge Narrativist folklore? Shoot him or indulge Narrativist folklore? The Reverend John Calvin Jenkins preserved his miserable life for the time being.

"The Sad House is a Narrativist sacred site, like Archelon Ranch. It's a place the author can't escape; at least part of him can't escape it. Every person stores their baggage somewhere inside them and since this place is somewhere inside the author it's therefore..."

"Someplace inside and *outside* of the book."

"Uh huh. So, if we reach the Sad House, there's a chance, just a chance that we might find the author or a piece of him at least, one that can be communicated with and convinced to help us."

I was excited. I could have the one who really made this happen tied up in the back of my van. I could force him to make this whatever kind of world I wanted it to be; a safe world, a kind world, a world where I was respected and acknowledged for my virtues. Everybody wants this kind of world. Everybody deserves this kind of world and maybe the author could give it to Bernard in Archelon Ranch, but he

GARRETT COOK

could give it to everyone if I got a hold of him. I drove
north, toward a better future.

VII

Bernard pushed himself harder than he had before. The deluge of bodies walking and the universe of possibilities made the Objectivity quiver with excitement, twitch in him and torment him. It screamed out vehemently for experiences, aching for new selves, but none of those selves at all was a self worth being. For example, there was the eyeless prostitute who had found some takers working the line. The Objectivity wanted to be another one of those takers in a much more meaningful and disgusting way. It wanted to not only savor the pleasure of the Harvester she was giving a blowjob to, but also the degradation of the disgusting eyeless cow giving the chitinous, insectoid member more respect than it looked like it deserved, and as the Harvester came after a lot of sucking and stroking the Objectivity insisted that Bernard had to be a sperm and that Bernard in fact was a sperm all along.

It moved onto processing the feelings of the comprachicos with their chain gangs of feral West Side street kids and then insisted that Bernard had to know what it was to be a feral West Side street kid inside out. Too many selves gathered in one place, chattering in their inane, grotesque, oppressed minds. Come on, it's not so great being you. You're not you. How could you be you? I am Bernard, I am Bernard. He had to focus on the image of his hands; make them clear. The Objectivity was blurring his connection with his body, spinning through elements of others like a slot machine. I am Bernard, I am Bernard, I am Bernard. Another hat. A strange influx of French. Je ne suis pas un chapeau, je suis un homme. Je suis Bernard. The Objectivity gave up, though it clearly did not wish to. The desire to remain Bernard was far too strong to beat as Chuck Calloway bought him an ice cream cone, which he ate with gusto and appreciation.

"Thanks," said Bernard, "it's awfully hot."

The fan platform above them kicked on and soon afterward the mallgoing scum enjoyed a few minutes of relief from the extraordinary heat they lived under. It did not stop them from beating the children they had up for sale or from pleasuring Johns but their appreciation could be felt. The line began to move as one of the more monstrously fat and sweaty of the patrons of the line cooled down enough to take the three steps he needed to make it to the entrance. It would likely be only a few more hours until Bernard could get in, since there were just another couple of thousand mallgoers who needed to be checked for contraband, which included outside food and controversial reading materials. There wasn't anything else that could be called too shameful for the Mall. Still, the search was needlessly thorough and often ended with a bribe or someone getting shot. Bernard was excited that the line seemed to be thinning slightly, but still could do little more than continuously argue and assert his selfhood to his very insistent condition.

Finally, he reached the front of the line, where he was prodded, probed, questioned and threatened, though not in that order.

"Wow," Bernard said to Chuck, "this has got to be some mall."

When he entered, he saw that it was indeed some mall. The digital map of the entrance said there were "seventy five miles and three thousand floors of consumerific fun". The bottom floor near the entrance consisted mostly of low income housing and competing discount hot sauce outlets.

Even in this unholy heat, discount hot sauce remained extremely popular, with Boxcar Joe's and Boxcar Willie's TresChic Discount Hotsauce Emporiums at the top of the heap. Boxcar had remained the one dollar hot sauce of the rich and famous but Boxcar Willie's TresChic was the choice of the intelligentsia. The rivalry was getting wildly out of hand; Boxcar Willie was the fifth to bear the name and Boxcar Joe the third to bear his. Many of the low-income apartments had reinforced doors in case the two hotsauce giants started shooting again.

Chuck stuck close, sensing that his new friend was not particularly wise in the ways of the world, and knowing those who were not worldly or witty enough ended up facing great misfortune. There were a lot of ways this could happen; whether through the actions of rabid squatters looking to violate the "No Outside Food Rule" in a truly morbid fashion or through those of antisocial and unscrupulous merchants who would just as soon sell their customers into slavery as sell them their wares. Bernard scrolled through the floors on the digital map, but didn't look as if he was finding anything. Chuck put a fatherly hand on the young man's shoulder.

"Somethin' wrong, Bernard?"

"I can't see the way out, you know into the —"

Chuck gagged Bernard with his hand for a second.

"Don't say that. People will hear you. They herd out the Suburbanites, but other than that nobody really knows the way out there. Folks don't need to go to the you-know-whats."

"I do. I need to get out there really badly."

"Well, I know a place where there might be someone who can help you, but I can't guarantee anything."

Bernard's eyes lit up.

"Really? You know somebody like that?"

"I know *of* somebody like that and I gotta warn you, the two things are pretty different."

"Oh."

"But, I know where you can find him."

Chuck punched in Floor 360 on the digital map console, then typed in "Juliet's" and a large, automated cart drove up to them. There was a slot on it with a picture of Ralph Nader. Bernard's jaw dropped in disbelief. Everything here was a fortune. He inserted the Nader and they got into the cart which drove past thousands of ramshackle apartments, some too poor to afford a door so risking death in the hot sauce turf wars, homeless people roasting a pig on a pile of Boxcar Willie's TresChic flyers, fat people, fat people, more fat people and a discount hot sauce district any large city could be proud of, let alone a mall. The cart finally parked itself outside of an elevator, which Chuck called down by typing commands on yet another console.

The two boarded the elevator, which dispensed two liquifilm syringes for their convenience as it took quite awhile to get up 359 floors, especially with all of the stops it made. Chuck enjoyed the Three Stooges short, while Bernard refused. Liquifilm could cause permanent identity shifts in people suffering from severe Objectivity. If Bernard had decided to indulge, he would have spent the rest of his existence as Moe Howard. Even the presence of the liquifilm syringe was enough to cause giddiness in the Objectivity, causing him to very much want to poke the muscular comprachico standing next to him in the eye.

After approximately another forever, the elevator stopped at floor 360. The mall must have been built ascending into higher tawdriness, for if the first floor looked tawdry, then floor 360 looked 359 increments of tawdriness worse. Its theme was The Works of the Marquis De Sade, and it was taken quite seriously. The comprachico excitedly skipped his chain of young boys into a bookstore called Passolini's. The Objectivity sought to play a dreadful prank on Bernard but the obvious gravity of the situation had Bernard holding onto his identity for dear life.

Other red-lit boutiques and bars offered their promises of flesh and experience that the Objectivity smelled and longed for as well. It wanted to know what it was to be a cat-of-nine-tails raking across an old man's back, the doubleheaded dildo shared by two curious college roommates, the Plexiglass on a peepshow booth. The condition which those who were bold enough to try Mud/CRAMPS variations said was a pinnacle of wisdom was like a distracted child taunted by a universe of toys and candy. It smelled potential and potential was all it cared about.

They passed the senior's center and walked some time until they came to a black curtain that smelled of rose perfume and sweet secretions. Above it hung a modest sign with humble calligraphy announcing that behind this curtain was Justine's. The Objectivity made supersonic screams, howled and clawed like wild baboons and flared up with solar heat. The "I am Bernard" assertion was as loud as Bernard could make it and it felt like but a whisper compared to the demands of the Objectivity. He had an odd desire to be that curtain, innocent yet wholly aware of whatever vices might be indulged behind it. Life as a black velvet curtain wouldn't be all that awful, yet as he said to the Objectivity many times, there were things to do as Bernard now. To the Objectivity's credit, this was the first offer since reaching the mall that actually tempted him.

When he walked through the curtain, he was greeted by a young woman whose black leather bodysuit clung to her as if it feared being blown away and never seeing her again. Bernard was reminded of the golden-haired ladies of Archelon Ranch, of the mint green girl and her tight, smooth body, of the young woman that drank him when he was a martini. They were all beautiful; all amazing in their way, but the leather girl impressed him for reasons that were entirely unique. In a world with so much suffering, she had chosen to suffer, constraining herself with a tight leather costume in spite of the desperate heat. She was wholly unlike everyone else who would rush toward the fanbreezes during cooling time. They had risked suffering only for the prospect of relief and comfort. Bernard, having suffered at the hands of his father, his brother and Professor Sagramour had wished to never suffer again, hence the drive to reach Archelon Ranch. She had decided she would. She must have possessed great power and wisdom. She moved him as much philosophically as she stimulated him erotically. What a fantastic creature!

"You must be hot in there."

"It's air conditioned. There are Freon jets inside it. Technically illegal."

As she said it, she got less beautiful and fascinating. He noticed that her nose was too long and hawkish and there were blotches of acne on her right cheek. Nothing was all that impressive about her. Still, he almost gave into the Objectivity's sudden desire to be that body suit, to be close to her, to bathe in her sweat and drink the juices between her legs. He felt as hot as he had initially thought she was and much more uncomfortable as he entered Justine's.

The place was unlike any other place he'd been before. There were tables of various sizes here, like the restaurant, but they were different, some of them were long, surgical and steely like the table

Sagramour strapped him to for experiments. People were bound to these too but it didn't look like they were test subjects. There were upright leather cushions against the wall and people were bound to them as well. Taking up half the room was a round stage on which several women were dancing. Each felt quite special. He sat down at a table near the stage and watched.

A corseted Suburbanite, probably early in the transformation, was placing pins in the hide of a very sultry lady Harvester. There was a look of pure satisfaction in her eyes as she, who had lived a life where sensations were dulled by her chitinous skin, discovered what it was to feel pain. In gratitude, she offered the Suburbanite thirsty kisses which dripped green mud down her chin. The Suburbanites eyes rolled back in her head and she was elsewhere, somewhere exquisite and dangerous. The Objectivity yanked him toward her, but corrected itself, knowing it could not share the things Suburbanites knew. Bernard was relieved for he feared this would have certainly been a springboard into Total Objectivity.

Dancing beside the bizarre couple was something Bernard did not even know existed. His brother had told him about these things, but his father had assured him they could not be. There was a real live Slaughterer on the stage! As designer humans were being developed, some to survive the heat, others to be able to take in toxic substances (Bernard was an impressive variation on those), they created another strain to put mankind on par with junglecats, gila-walruses and dinosaurs. Incorporating jaguar and snake DNA, these perfect assassins were supposed to be the best line of defense humanity could muster, but the Slaughterers turned out wrong; they became almost like the Suburbanites, entities of uncontrolled libido who could think of little but utilizing their special pheromones to find prospective mates. The Slaughterer swayed in ways that human beings were not supposed to, especially human beings built with curves as thick as hers. Her jet black nipples stroked the thirsty and curious parts of Bernard's mind. They looked all the more fleshy and tender on her spotted, silky hide. He felt something electric and she leaned down from the stage and licked him on the forehead with her long, forked serpent's tongue.

"Mmmm…" she moaned.

The Slaughterer got down on her hands and knees, grinding hard against the stage and began to purr loudly. She pushed her soft, furry breasts into Bernard's face rubbing hi. The purring grew louder as he opened his mouth and took in a soft, black hard nipple. The purring disappeared abruptly and the Slaughterer let out a loud growl. Bernard just barely escaped from the wide-open fanged mouth by twitching in his seat.

"Sorry, daddy," she purred, "I promise I'll be good. I'll be real good."

He leaned in once again, following the scent of the potent pseudopheromones coming off of the Slaughterer. The Slaughterer's excited wide-open smile became a frown as Chuck pulled Bernard away from her.

"She bites," Chuck told Bernard, in the same tone a parent explains not to touch the stove, "she's dangerous."

"She says she'll be good."

"No, daddy, I'll be good. Real good."

The purring was as loud as the revving of a truck as she grinded harder against the stage. Her eyes were wide and expectant. It was now no surprise to Bernard that people would deny the existence of Slaughterers. The creature was beautiful, but it was a disappointment as both killer and sex machine. On the other hand, Bernard couldn't really mock other beings for being a scientific disappointment as he himself was not performing his initial purpose, which had been to free mankind from the Suburbanite condition and render them immune to the mud. Something like that could not be a scientific failure any more than he could. The more he thought about it, identified with her and defended her, the more he wanted to touch her again, dangerous or not. That was what this place was about, wasn't it? The other women on the stage were wrestling, making out, letting snakes crawl all over them, but they were nowhere near as interesting as the Slaughterer.

Chuck grabbed Bernard and shook him.

"What?" Bernard's voice was that of a teenager roused for school.

"This isn't why I brought you here."

"Oh?"

"I brought you here to see the guy. Remember the guy?"

The call of Archelon Ranch began to drown out the pheromones. Blue sea. No suffering. No city. Beautiful, primal, real. Archelon Ranch is calling you home. I could be happy right here. The splendors of this place are nothing. The filth, the spots, the claws are meaningless. Archelon Ranch is truth and all else is a lie. Yes, remember the guy, the reason that brought you here.

"Yeah, I remember. Can you introduce me to this guy?"

Chuck shrugged.

"I don't know. Maybe when the waitress comes around she can tell us who he is."

Their waitress' name was Cindy, like the proprietor of the diner. It was a common name in food service. Bernard could tell because it was written across her bare chest in cuts that attracted almost as much attention as the vampire fangs in her mouth and the World War One German army helmet on her head.

"Something I can do for you boys?"

Bernard nodded.

"I'll take a synth-berry carbobev."

"Far out. That's law, kid, fuckin' law."

Most people would have sighed or shook their heads knowing they were sitting with somebody who would order synth-berry carbobev at a place like this and been frustrated by Bernard's babe-in-the-woods tendencies, but Chuck Calloway was a patient man, a man who met a terrifying city with gentle good humor every morning. He didn't say a word to Bernard, didn't laugh at him. He beckoned the waitress closer.

"Can I find The Whisper here?"

The waitress almost swallowed her fake vampire fangs. It was a name she hadn't expected to hear.

"I'm sorry. Never heard of him."

"The Whisper. Don't pretend like you don't know him. I know that he comes here."

"Ooh, I don't know if I should…"

Chuck touched her arm and looked up into her eyes.

"My friend here has been through a lot and has a long way to go. We need this guy's help. If you could find the kindness and generosity in your heart to help him out, I'd sure appreciate it."

The waitress tapped her foot nervously.

"Well, okay," she said, and pointed to an upright surgical table resting against the walls. Automated hands were burning a naked man with lit cigarettes. Chuck shook his head in disbelief. "I tell you, Cindy, it takes all kinds."

Cindy laughed. "Don't I know it."

Chuck and Bernard walked up to the man. He sneered at them.

"What the Hell do you want? Do I look like a man who would want anybody's company, let alone a couple of assholes like yourselves?"

"Are you The Whisper?" Chuck asked, leaning very close.

"Yeah, maybe I am. What's it to you?"

"We need to know something."

"And?"

Bernard couldn't hear what Chuck whispered in the man's ear, but his eyes grew wide with anticipation. Bernard had a feeling he didn't want to know.

"What do you need me to tell you?" The Whisper asked.

"The best way to get out to the west suburbs."

The Whisper leaned forward as much as the metal restraints allowed.

"You go to any elevator, you type sub-basement C. They'll ask for a password, which is a semi-colon. Just type a semi-colon."

"Thanks."

"No problem."

Bernard hadn't met anybody who seemed to know so much so decided to take advantage while he could.

"Have you ever heard of Archelon Ranch?"

"I know very little about it, I'm afraid. I only know that it's a sort of paradise, but if you're asking about it, I imagine you'd already know that, right?"

"Yeah, I know that, I think," Bernard replied.

"Then I'm sorry, cause I can't tell you anything else."

Bernard finished his carbobev, sucking blue spots off the ice. He would have ordered another, but he knew it would have come across as a transparent attempt to catch more of the show. Archelon Ranch was out there though. He was sure there would be better things to look at there. They found an elevator panel and Chuck punched in the strange sequence of buttons. This elevator came up faster than the others even, leaping up eagerly to pick up the two VIPs. Chuck plunged in a liquifilm of *Un Chien Andalou* and enjoyed the ride, while Bernard distracted himself from the Objectivity and the pull of the liquifilm by reading one of the Jack London novels programmed into his genetic code. Between the Andalucian dog that wasn't in the film and scrappy White Fang, the wolf dog won out.

They got off at Sub-basement C and it was not what Bernard expected. Several cooing, barking, trembling, writhing Suburbanites were magnetized to a black-tinted plexiglass wall. Chuck and Bernard treaded lightly, careful to avoid the little pools of rotten, petrified mud that the incapacitated but deadly subhumans spat up. Because they were doing this, they were walking when they should have definitely been running, dashing for their lives instead of cautiously creeping around. Though they avoided the mud, they were not able to avoid the Standardizers that were dropping down from secret panels in the ceiling to deal with intruders and criminals.

Standardizers were the fourth and worst kind of designer human. Most of their mutations came from ratel DNA. Before the gilawalruses were created and subsequently unleashed, the ratel looked very impressive. The ratel, or honey badger, is native to the Indian subcontinent and some parts of Africa, although it could probably survive wherever it likes. Ratels attack beehives for the honey inside, unaffected by stings on account of their coarse fur. They eat turtles by burrowing through their shells with their sharp claws. They are unafraid of snakes and kill and eat them often. They are known to kill other animals, take over their burrows and surprise unfortunate members of that animal's family and slaughter them. All of these traits were taken into consideration when creating Standardizers to cleanse the suburbs. From the way these Standardizers held Sub-basement C, it was clear they were pretty effective.

These Standardizers were not just here to cleanse Suburbanites. They glowed semaphore at each other (a product of fiery phosphorescence in their DNA) and pulled out syringe launchers. From the bluegreen color of the liquid in their syringes, Bernard could tell they had been told there was an

Objective around. The syringes were loaded with liquifilm.

You are Groucho Marx. You are Bugs Bunny. You are a cartoon jellyfish. You are Claude Rains. You are battling a maneating tarantula. You are five tacos for a nickel. You are a talking helicopter. Dizzy. Stupid. Too much noise. He pulled the gun from his shirt pocket and felt for his targets. Though he was pulled by the liquifilm, he still understood the Standardizers and their place, when they'd move, how they'd move, almost why they'd move. He dodged the liquifilm that they launched and peppered them with bullets.

But he had not accounted for the synthetic ratel mutation. Just as beestings were to the scrappy, vicious honey badger, so were bullets to the Standardizers; they didn't even break the skin. They sidled into formation, blinking news at one another. Hateful, arrogant smiles dominated their grey, furry faces. Fast as Bernard moved, he couldn't outrun the lure of the Objectivity. He was doomed now for his transgressions against society, defying Professor Sagramour who had been the one to invent Standardizers. He would have been doomed, that is, had Chuck not decided to do something admirable, beautiful and stupid. Chuck ran to the first control panel he saw and began buffeting it with his fists. One of the Standardizers blinked a pink warning at his comrades, but it wasn't quick enough. Chuck had damaged the control panel, and in doing so, he had demagnetized the Suburbanites.

Three of the green, slobbering aberrations showed their appreciation to Chuck by gnawing on his arms. All the rest seemed to understand that it was the Standardizers who had sealed them in, to keep them away from eating, fucking and spewing mud as they wished. The Standardizers dove into the fray, seeing the native species they had deceived contesting territory and forgot all about Bernard. Bernard turned to fire at the Suburbanites who were targeting Chuck, but it was too late. Bernard may have had a lot of ammo on him, but there was no sense wasting it. Chuck was dead.

As he rushed out the door into the suburbs, Bernard wished he'd had a moment to thank his first real friend for his sacrifice, but he did not, for he now had a vast, scary world to comprehend, a place that he hoped was not far from Archelon Ranch.

VIII

Sooner or later I knew that I would have to deal
with it; I would have to trust the Reverend enough to
untie him without assuming he would simply wander
off and disappear into the mall crowd. Although a lot
of people are escorted into the Mall bound, I would
not be able to do so with the Reverend for he was
enough of a public figure that it would look inappro-
priate or perhaps even suspicious. I undid the ropes,
pocketed the gun and led him to the extremely long
line knowing all I could do was hope for the best.
Maybe the Reverend would decide that it was in his
best interest for me to have faith in him. He was
perverse like that. Sneaky too, which is why I didn't
bother injecting a liquifilm.

"You know," he said, "I could just run away."

"Yeah, I know."

"So why are you untying me?"

"Cause sooner or later I'm going to have to, so it
might as well be now."

"I guess that's true."

I yawned. After making the concession of untying the Reverend, it was a bit too big of a chink in

my tough guy kidnapper defenses, so I motioned to a
nearby Supra-Adderall tea vendor.

"I'll take one of the big ones," I told him, "one of
the real big ones."

He held up a 90 ounce cup. That was too big.

"No, not that big. Smaller than that."

We argued through five more sizes before I ended
up having to admit that it was the small I had wanted
all along. I felt like a seven year old, but 90 ounces
of hot Supra-Adderall tea could possibly kill me. Supra-Adderall was in most beverages, but I knew that
this stuff was not particularly refined. The bits of pill
floating in it were a dead giveaway. When you're in
line at the Mall, you have to avoid purchasing the sort
of things you can only purchase in line at the Mall.

"You want any?" I asked the Reverend. He nodded emphatically.

"I'll take the large."

I felt a bit sick. Was he attempting suicide?

"That stuff can kill you, you know."

"So could the gun you had to my head not five
minutes ago. Sometimes, you need to take risks. Besides, my secretary brews me a pot of this stuff every
morning. I've been waiting eagerly for them to finally
upgrade to Supra-Adderall 8. I've got videogames to
beat, so I need to clot fast."

I sipped my sensibly-sized tea as he eagerly gulped
down his tower of pharmaceutical voodoo. He looked
like an orang with a heroin needle. The only differ-
ence was I tended not to stand next to the orangs
shooting up an emasculatingly small amount while
they went through needle after needle. The growl of
semi-human satisfaction he emitted was no different
than theirs. If I had reason to be annoyed with myself
for accepting this man's religious precepts before, I
had reason to be deeply embarrassed now. He licked
particles of Supra-Adderall 7 off his lid as I took my
third sip. "Pussy", he said with his eyes. "Junky" mine
replied.

"You'd better not run," I blurted out. Three sips and I was already a tiny bit twitchy.

"I won't."

"You swear? You swear cause if you run, I'll..."

"I swear, I fuckin' swear man. Honest? What do you want?"

"You'd better not be lying, cause if you're lying..."

He shook his head and began doing jumping-jacks in place.

"I swear to you Clyde, on the holy name of Garrett Cook that I am not under any circumstances going to run away, no matter how tempting it seems. Most importantly, Clyde, I swear on the name of Garrett Cook that I will not give you a reason to shoot me, no matter how tempting it would be. And I swear to you on the name of Garrett Cook that I'm in fact a little bit excited about this venture."

"You've always wanted to go to the Sad House, haven't you?"

"Uh huh."

I had an epiphany. Well not an epiphany. One of those things that's just like it in the way that a pygmy hippo is like a regular hippo. I don't think there's a word for them.

"And you don't think you could survive the Mall and the suburbs alone, do you? You're not going to run away because you need me here. You don't need me to kill you, there's a whole deadly world outside the city to do it for you..."

"Plot preserve, just put in your fucking liquifilm."

I did just that, putting in my favorite bootleg George Meliés porno. A tall blackhaired young woman, with the kind of figure that would make a girl nowadays think she was too fat to live, wandered through a cardboard forest under a jolly, bearded, laughing sun. She looked nervous at first, but then got calm, looking up and sharing a smile with the benevolent old man in the sky. Suddenly, huge card-board phalluses rose up from the ground. She leapt over one after another, then knelt down and stroked each cardboard cock as though it were a loveable capricious little animal of some kind. She laughed, then kissed them and wrapped her arms around them. Then things changed. The sun abruptly stopped laughing. The coming change was sort of scary. The sun let out a silent scream as it was yanked away by a rope from above it. The girl put her hand over her mouth as it cut to a title card.

"Oh my! Whatever has happened?"

Another title card comes up. It is simple, blunt and ominous.

"Night has fallen."

Cut back to the forest. The sun has been replaced by a moon with a lean, wicked bitter face. A pair of tiny spectacles dangles off the edge of old, bitter, awful mister moon's sharp nose. A curtain on which is projected a closeup of a hot, wet vagina falls behind the trees. A woman in a wolf costume creeps up on the girl, making sure to take time to slink between each cardboard tree as she does so. If Meliés' porn had been available in the twentieth century you would think the wolf lady was an inspiration for the costume in Sendak's *Where the Wild Things Are*. The girl holds onto one of her phallus friends for dear life and protection, trembling.

Cut to title card.

"These woods are savage and awful at night!"

Cut back to the forest and the "wolf" whose arms are raised threateningly.

Title card. "Grr, I'm going to get you!"

Title card. "No, please! Don't!" The wolf doesn't listen and the girl can't get away. The wolf throws her down, kisses her greedily and tongues her nipples. She puts a wolfy hand between the girl's legs as she begins to gently bite her breasts. The girl does not look excited by this. She is still frightened, horrified in fact, but does nothing to resist. She can't. The wolf-woman and the angry moon are powerful, too evil for innocence to conquer. The girl begins to cry. There is a very modern closeup on her face as a tear runs down her cheek. After this momentary breach of style that sometimes makes me doubt the authenticity of the bootleg, the elegant rape resumes and the wolf-woman kisses gently down the girl's belly.

Title card. "You're mine now! Mine forever!"

"No!"

"You are my princess and you belong to me!"

In the forest, the wolfwoman inserts her tongue. Another breach of style follows; a closeup on the girl as more tears stream down her cheek and she gives out a silent scream of pure desperation. Her thick lipstick and her running eye makeup render the experience ecstatic. It makes up for the anachronistic shot.

The moon shares her scream. The old man face is filled with despair and then fuming with anger.

Title card. "No! NO! NOOOOO!!!!!"

The wire hoists up the moon into nothingness, then brings down the sun. As if by magic, the wolf-woman's suit is gone and she holds hands with the girl. They laugh silent laughs, frolicking in the phallic forest without the threat of the pussy curtain behind them. They embrace, and then play leapfrog, bouncing merrily over the phalluses, hugging, kissing and soothing the precious flowers. They kiss once more and share an embrace as a dick sprouts up between them.

Title card. "Life in the enchanted forest is sweet. But watch out for wolves!"

Title card. "The End".

Since this is good, laboratory grade liquifilm this plays forty times before it's done. I emerge from the enchanted forest to find myself almost at the front of the line, just as I suspected I would be. The Reverend is standing beside me. His recent revelation wasn't an attempt to trick me into distracting myself so he could run away. He is practicing Jeet Kun Do moves.

The Supra-Adderall 7 he's ingested seems to show no signs of wearing off. We move through the line and the contraband Iguanodon stops at the guy in front of me. It emits a loud squawk and gives a spiky thumbs-down. The guard looks the guy over and finds a banana stashed in his speedo. It might be to impress the ladies, but that doesn't stop it from being contraband.

"No outside food!" the guard shouted, shooting the guy in the neck. I was grateful that I only brought firearms, chloroform and a gas mask and neither outside food or controversial reading material as either of those two things would be flat out suicidal in the Mall. The security guard tipped his helmet to the Reverend and the Reverend in turn waved hello. He finally stood still for a second.

"Plot preserve, Reverend!" said the security guard.

"Plot preserve, Julio."

"I heard, Reverend," Julio whispered, "I heard."

He couldn't keep his volume down for long.

"I'm just amazed! I feel so much hope and purpose and I am so privileged to be with you in these fantastic times. Welcome to the mall, Reverend!" he hugged the Reverend almost to the point of constriction, then let go.

"Is this the guy? Oh my god, is he? Plot fucking preserve! It's the protagonist!"

"No, my son," the Reverend replied, getting a bit green. The mere notion must have been enough to start to send the Supra-Adderall tea back up. I was offended, but I could see where he was coming from. I was, however, frustrated that Bernard's clumsy ascension into the role hadn't gotten the same response out of him. He had just been incredulous when I first presented the theory, not sickened like he was with the implication that I could have been the protagonist. If I were a violent man and the guard were not a Narrativist with a gun, I'd have given the Reverend a good solid smack. Okay, I am a violent man, but the guard was a Narrativist with a gun, so I couldn't give the Reverend a good solid smack.

"I'm sorry, Reverend," the security guard said, looking deeply contrite and red with embarrassment, "I just figured you would be guiding the you-know to you-know-where. I didn't know you were simply going shopping with your friend."

"No, the you-know is not with me nor, lamentably, shall he ever be."

The security guard went from apologetic to quite scared.

"We're doing something, aren't we? I can't imagine not helping him out. If we don't, then what purpose do we have? There are Standardizers out there, you know."

The Reverend dismissed the security guard's concerns immediately.

"Of course we're doing something for him, my son. You should have more faith in me. We've set him up with a fairly substantial sum of money and Chuck Callaway's with him. He'll be okay. Not that he needs the help, mind you. He is the you-know."

"Yes, certainly. He doesn't need it."

"Are we done here, Julio?"

"Yes, Reverend of course. Plot preserve."

The Reverend stopped himself. In his hopped up state, he'd almost forgotten something important.

"Sub-basement C, right?"

"No, it's D here. We had to tunnel underneath the lair of the noble gilawalrus."

"Lovely creature, the gilawalrus."

"Plot preserve the gilawalrus."

"Plot preserve the gilawalrus."

Narrativists have a bizarre attachment to the gilawalrus, believing it to be one of the author's wisest and most capable creations. I was pretty certain even during my time as a devout Narrativist that they were nothing more than poisonous child-eating vermin with no sensible ecological niche. But, whatever.

I didn't feel like arguing about this particularly silly piece of Narrativist dogma as debating it would make it look like I hadn't flat out dismissed all of Narrativism, which I had.

As the Reverend and I walked into the Mall, I was full of questions. There might very well have been a lot of information exchanged in that conversation and none of it was for me. As the kidnapper and the mind behind this pilgrimage, this bothered me plenty. I deserved to know something. I deserved in particular to know about Bernard and his prospects. Maybe in a roundabout way I could get something out of him. I had heard the name Chuck Callaway before. Maybe he had been at the church or maybe he had a reputation at the Mall.

"Who's Chuck Callaway?" I asked, making sure it sounded like nothing but idle curiosity.

"Chuck Callaway is one of my best men, one of my first converts. He's a former English Professor turned private detective. He's playing a benevolent truck driver who has his ear to the street. It's a cliché, but Chuck doesn't mind, he'll do anything for the cause. If there's anybody who will get through this alive, it'll be Chuck, he's brave, tough as nails and surprisingly quick; really puts the odds in our favor."

"But you don't know how he's doing."

"Of course not. I have no communication with him."

"Are you sure that's really the way to go, Reverend? It sounds awfully risky to me. "

He shook his head.

"Not going to risk it. Chuck's the guy. Chuck will make it. I can't compromise the narrative like that. Besides, my plan stopped you, didn't it?"

I really wanted to beat the arrogant smirk off his face, but he was being really useful. Maybe I preferred him useless, though; I could torture him and abuse him with no ramifications that way.

"So what exactly is Sub-basement D?"

"Narrativist holy sites are usually unknown locations beyond the suburbs, right?"

"Yes."

"So, it goes without saying that someday Narrativists might need access to the suburbs. So, we've hacked into the security panels at the Mall in order to assure us future suburb access through any entrance."

"Ah."

As we entered the vast glassy lobby of the Mall, the Reverend approached a security console and in-putted the location and the floor and the elevator came when it was called as elevators tend to. We got in and I injected my liquifilm again, preferring my movie to the watered down shit they have in elevator liquifilm trays. I smiled my way through the perverse enchanted forest until the elevator stopped. The Reverend had to shake me out at the fortieth viewing, which made me feel like kind of a hypocrite for berating his Supra-Adderall habit. At least you can move and think on Supra-Adderall.

At first, the Sub-basement with its odd array of captured Suburbanites chained to the walls made me want to stop and gawk, but it didn't take me long to figure out that I'd be better off running like Hell for the door and pulling down my gasmask, before the Standardizers came down on me and ripped me to shreds. I had no interest at all in a run-in with Standardizers. The first phosphorescent glimmer of their presence I saw would make me shit my shorts. I handed the Reverend the pistol from my backpack as I took out the shotgun and caulked it.

As we stepped out of the mall and into the sub-urbs, the Reverend looked quite concerned.

"Thanks for the gun and all, Clyde, but I think there's a problem."

"What kind of problem?" I snarled. I really didn't need his bullshit as I began my exploration of one of the most dangerous places on earth.

"I don't have a gasmask."

It was an excellent point. In my zeal to rush out and kidnap the Reverend, I had neglected to pack a second gas mask. If it hadn't rained recently and we were careful about not making prolonged physical contact with any freshly bred mud, there would be no problems. Hopefully. Maybe. Okay, I fucked up completely. This wasn't good at all. I think my mistake was mostly in expecting that this man would be dead and therefore out of my hair completely by now. Who'd have known he would prove himself so useful to me? Damn. I almost felt like apologizing. Almost and not very much.

"Just don't breathe any of the gases the mud emits when water hits it and don't step in wet mud and you'll be fine. Especially if it hasn't and doesn't rain."

"Well, if it's so safe traipsing through the suburbs, maybe you'd like to relinquish that gas mask."

"Hey! I gave you a gun in case the Suburbanites show up. It's much more than I, as a kidnapper and heretic, am really obligated to do."

"You're an idiot. Give me the fucking gasmask."

"No."

"Fuck you. Give me the mask."

"No, I'm not gonna breathe that shit."

"It's your fault I don't have a mask, so you should give me yours."

"Fuck you!"

"Fuck you, too!"

"Fuck you more!"

There was a sudden silence between us as we both fully processed where we were. The suburbs were a mythic and mysterious place, horrible as they were, and our bickering would only serve to dilute the experience. It wasn't a nightmare world right now. There was no gas cloud, the Suburbanites were all inside, the mud was old and hard and dead, far from the organic slimy obstacle fresh mud could be. The only sound was the cackling of hundreds of laughtracks from inside the houses. I was sad that these creatures had to live out here and didn't even know about liquifilm. Then again, Suburbanites didn't exactly have high standards for what constituted entertainment. It made me feel bad about all the times I'd injected that mud into my brother for the experiments. The last four times were, of course, to progress his escape, but every other time it had been nothing but leisure, a way to pass an afternoon before a liquifilm buy.

It was beyond simple cruelty on my part. It was completely inhuman. Mud is the off switch for the Superego and the Ego, the big maybe. It says "maybe human flesh tastes good", "maybe you are a rhinoceros", "maybe everything that you wished was true about this world is right and nothing has been stopping you from becoming omnipotent but an invisible schoolmarm who just wants to cramp your style because she's jealous." How dare she cramp your style. How dare your body tell you you aren't a rhinoceros. How dare your conscience tell you you can't eat your own child. That's why my brother began to develop Deep Objectivity as a coping mechanism — an anti-venom. I had a shot of CRAMPS in my backpack, but enough mud and that wouldn't do a whole shit load of good. I went full circle to the Reverend and the danger he'd be in again. I'm one of those people who can't get up in the morning without wronging somebody somehow. I probably should have stayed at the mall, just right for me: the end point of human culture, the last people place for somebody who barely had humanity in him.

As he had on the elevator, the Reverend shook me out of my funk. In spite of the answers that only come at the edge of being, we were still wandering the very same utter wasteland of petrified hallucinogenic mud I was guilty for sending the Reverend into without proper protection. He was over his anger at me and now intent upon surviving. He was surprisingly on top of everything.

"We have to head north until the mud stops," he told me, "when the mud stops, we'll know we're there."

"How will we know that?" I asked.

He got that look on his face that people give you when you ask for directions to the street you're walking down.

"Because the mud is an authorial conceit. Narrativism has declared sacred any place that blurs the boundaries of authorial conceit. Archelon Ranch and the Sad House both do this. The Sad House, I must warn you, will be strange and terrible. It is a gathering place for demons in the author's psyche that he cannot defeat. Going there, will mean experiencing the broken parts of the author and feeling temporary objectivity."

"Good. I've always been jealous of Bernard's objectivity."

"That's one of the stupidest things I've ever heard."

I knew full well that it was, but I didn't dare say it. It was bad enough that I knew I had no good reason to envy that part of my brother. Objectivity might actually be worse than being a Suburbanite, although I've been told that an Objective at least can't be turned into a Suburbanite, so I guess it has that edge.

"I'm sorry," said the Reverend, actually meaning it, "it must be extremely hard for you."

"It is."

The next thing the Reverend said surprised me, "It's hard for me too. I do everything I can to keep the narrative pure, but I know that due to Garrett Cook's personal disdain for metafiction, something as stupid as a Church of Authorial Intent really looks like a bad idea. You and I are actually in the same position, only I believe in the book and you don't. Otherwise things are exactly alike for us."

I began to like the Reverend John Calvin Jenkins again. He began to feel like a friend. A friend who I had kidnapped and dragged on a mysterious journey into a world of horrors on the off chance that I could prevent my brother from fulfilling his purpose in life, which is a unique kind of friend that I don't think anyone else could boast.

"Sorry I kidnapped you and forgot your gas mask."

"Sorry your worthless brother's the protagonist."

A drop of water plopped against the Reverend's head.

"I'm sorry it's starting to rain and Suburbanites are attracted to the scent of gas."

We laughed together for some reason as the rain began to come down and doors of nearby houses began to open. A ragged band of Suburbanites stepped outside to breathe in the gas and go about their baffling daily routines. A naked man with long grey hair beat a fat man with a guitar. The fat man was chewing on pieces of insulation. A girl in a raggedy cheerleader uniform was led out on a leash by a shirtless clown whose chest was covered in scars. A man dressed only in a catcher's mask sodomized a priest. A bald man in a business suit swung a broadsword back and forth as two twin brothers gnawed on each other. A teenager in dirty khakis finished strangling a middle-aged woman in a skirt and tight sweater and stared at us hungrily. Their lives were nothing but a continuous cycle of eating, fucking, beating and wanting and they found nothing wrong with dragging intruders into it.

"Just do me a favor and shoot my ass," said the Reverend, "I'm startin' to see things."

"I don't know if I can, Reverend." I probably couldn't. Why couldn't I have kept hating this man?

"It was the best of times it was the worst of times."

He stood there staring into space as the group of Suburbanites descended on him. He did nothing as the guitar smacked him in the head and as the cheerleader reached under his robes, pulled out his penis and started gnawing it. I blasted her, then the clown. The businessman with the broadsword charged me screaming, "Have at it, knave!" and I did, shooting him in the chest. I blasted Suburbanites as the Reverend scribbled in the air, spending his time doing the one thing he had subconsciously always wanted to do. I shot him too along with every other Suburbanite I could. Some of them backed off, but the fat man was on him. I shot him, but knew I was only delaying the inevitable. Suburbanites fuck and eat their dead and there were enough of them in town that I'd run out of ammunition before I could stop them. Even as I spent the last of my shells, the last one left alive, the one in the Abercrombie and Fitch shirt and cum and mud stained khakis kept at me. I dropped the shotgun, picked up the Reverend's pistol and began to head north as fast as my boots allowed me.

As two more doors burst open, I got a terrible feeling that I wasn't going to make it. They fell on me. I shot them off, quick as I could, but they were yanking at my gas mask, and I couldn't save it any more than I could have saved the Reverend. I ran and shot, ran and shot, but I couldn't flee the gas and my dark, ecstatic dreams.

I was a stiff cardboard cock springing up from the ground, satisfied with life under a beautiful cardboard sun with a big smile on its face, a loving gentle master that Garrett Cook had never offered before. The nude, dark haired girl frolicked joyfully among the penises here, unhampered by clothing, ethics or responsibility. She licked me, kissed me and ran her tongue down my whole cardboard length. She smiled, put her hands on her lips in a "shhhh, don't tell" gesture and sat down on me, taking my whole cardboard girth inside her. There was a warm, happy sun overhead and a warm pussy around me. I could no longer remember ever being a part of that stupid, godforsaken city that Garrett Cook had built to punish us. Almost. The unreality hit me fast. I felt this world's negative potential all at once and on a chain of semicolons the happy sun was yanked away and replaced by the scowling face of the moon.

I had never seen the face of Garrett Cook before, but I knew this had to be him. Nobody else had such dreadful power over my world; nobody else could make me suffer so much for so little reason. With the moon, the wolf appeared. It was Bernard in the wolf suit, slicing the naked girl to ribbons with very real and sharp claws, splattering her blood and insides all over the place. He laughed silently as he turned those claws on me, seeking to destroy my cardboard body.

Somewhere in there, I found myself. I thought of what I'd wanted from life, how I'd sought to get it and who I was. I thought about how this world offered me even less than the real one and the enchanted forest grew blurry. I found my body and reached into the backpack, actively denying the enchanted forest as I did so and took out the syringe of CRAMPS. I calmed myself, counted to one hundred in my head and re-minded myself that Suburbanites were here, some of them willing to kill me if I hesitated or did anything other than run or shoot. Run and Shoot. Those were the two components of my reality, the two things anchoring me to the earth and keeping me out of the enchanted forest until the CRAMPS set in.

As soon as I had the presence of mind to think of anything but running and shooting, I pulled the pins on two grenades and tossed them back at the angry suburbs. I fought in my head to maintain the existential integrity of the hell I was fleeing and to destroy the devils that came out of it at the same time. This place had destroyed my friend who had sought nothing more than to understand life and to feel important in it. I left behind a graveyard of sweat-shirts, business suits, sweaters, khakis, fetish wear and sporting equipment, the last traces of people that had no personhood. The further away from the sub-urbs I got, the further I got from the pull of the gas. I felt a sudden feeling of both purpose and aimlessness, the kind of freedom that would paralyze a man who did not know he was a fictional character that wasn't even supposed to be part of this narrative. I walked off the edge of the story, no more city, Mall, suburbs or book.

IX

Nothing had felt as wrong to Bernard as the suburbs. It was too quiet here. He had gotten used to the hustle and bustle, the noise, the psyches calling out for him to experience them, the objects to comprehend. There might have been walls and chimneys and doors, yes, and behind those walls, couches and televisions, but the Objectivity did not want this, the closeness to the Suburbanites was too much. Bernard was forced once more to deal only in his own experiences. It was disgusting.

I am Bernard and I am Bernard yet again and I am Bernard. He could think of nothing but survival, nothing more than the future of being Bernard. At Archelon Ranch Bernard shall be happy though Bernard is not at all happy now. Archelon Ranch couldn't be far, could it? If it was the future of being Bernard, then it was a torturous thing to deal with. Surely Archelon Ranch lay ahead as it was important to go west through the Mall out into the world, part of which had to be Archelon Ranch. He tried to feel nothing more than the call to Archelon Ranch, but he had other things to feel, things that were not at all pleasant.

He experienced the feeling someone gets to feel when they wonder why someone else had suffered. He had felt a multitude of sufferings, but not many that he could connect to himself and none as acutely connected to him as this one now. What exactly was it about Bernard that made somebody else willing to suffer for him? He could not think of anything in particular that he had ever done for anybody. The only thing that could have been considered beneficial was suffering through the tests that his father and Professor Sagramore had made him go through. He had been kind to science, but could think of nothing that he had done that was to the benefit of Chuck Callaway, especially nothing that would warrant Chuck dying for him. It was very unfair. Perhaps as unfair as Bernard's father had been toward him. Pity. What of all the people he had trampled while in his tyrannosaurus rex body? Pity. So many dead and none of them had deserved it, none but his father and Professor Sagramore. Those two had made him suffer, so it stood to reason that they deserved a measure of suffering themselves.

The only place with no suffering had to be Archelon Ranch, where he could go and feel and think of nobody's suffering and let the others who suffered make him suffer no more. Maybe the others suffered because he was made to survive mud injections, built to be special. Since he was that special, he was made to reach Archelon Ranch. He was special enough that others suffered so that he could reach a place where he suffered no longer. He considered this, and decided he would not have minded feeling the sufferings of others here since he knew they suffered for a reason.

But inside the houses around him, the souls and psyches did not move. The things in here suffered silently, walked in pain and brought it on others with no purpose beyond that they had nothing better to do. He shuddered knowing that were he not so special, the mud injections could have done this to him. Nearly mindless, nearly soulless, they had killed Bernard's first friend, Chuck. He knew behind those walls they were moving and at any time they could come out and that they wanted nothing more than to make people hurt. He held the gun tight knowing he would need to fire it soon.

He walked past the houses, felt them inside and saw them looking out at him. What was keeping them? He got nervous, paranoid and extremely angry. He wanted them to come out so he could hurt them for indulging in nothing better than hurt. He thought that if they did not wish to come out and hurt him they might have thought that he was one of their own and this would not do. One of them waved at him. The one on the stage hadn't snarled at him or made an effort to attack him either, but that had just been a show. Some of them might have been harmless. All of them could be harmless. He didn't feel like trusting them. He was glad he hadn't when suddenly the Objectivity refused something. I am not a Suburbanite.

Refreshing thought, but what was not a refreshing thought was the meaning of Bernard's refusal and the catalyst of it. It was a teenager wearing a baseball jersey with no pants, his pale green manhood dangling out offensively. The jersey was covered in petrified mud and a few spots of something that definitely had to be blood. He fired the gun, shooting it in the eye and sending it flying. The feeling kept coming. I am not a Suburbanite. I am not a Suburbanite.

"Hello Jesus," said a stark naked old lady who was missing her right nipple, "mama's ready for you."

He fired the gun again, one shot. His shots were always perfect. This wouldn't be too difficult. An old man emerged from one of the houses. He pointed up at the heavens and bits of green meat came out of his mouth as he talked.

"Look up. When the poundcakes come down, it will be okay." One shot again this time. Bam. Down. I am not a Suburbanite. I am not a Suburbanite. A burly man in a plumber's uniform held up a dead cat on a string. There was blood on its anus and one of its eyeballs was pulp.

"Fix it! Fix it!" he screamed. One shot. Bam. Down. I am not a Suburbanite.

A tall, birdlike lady in a bloody wedding dress swung a katana in circles over her head.

"I have found it! The perfect turkey. Gobble gobble gobble gobble gobble gobble gobble gobble..." Bam. Down. I am not a Suburbanite.

A lovely, slender teenage girl dragged a radioflyer wagon full of heads behind her.

"I will trade you four for your moped. Four for just one. It's a good deal."

He aimed, squeezed the trigger. Click. Checked his pockets for ammo. Nothing. I am not a Suburbanite I am a Suburbanite I am not a Suburbanite. A well-muscled young man with skin that might once have been brown had a rotten chicken on his left hand which was he was using as a puppet. Behind him, a four hundred pound woman wearing only an apron brandished a pair of hedge clippers. Behind her a green tinged Harvester was lining up a golf club to take a swing at her skull. A one legged old man behind the Harvester was trying idly to jump rope. The young man with the chicken puppet grabbed Bernard with his free hand and lifted him up. His strength was amazing and he was able to toss Bernard onto the girl's wagon. The girl jumped up and down and applauded.

"Five?" she asked.

"You're not going to take my son," the strong young man answered, almost replying to what she was saying.

The gigantic woman with the hedge clippers plunged them into the once brown young man's back.

He wobbled, shifted, almost lost balance, but his well-muscled calves held up.

"You're not going to take my son!"

"Five!"

"You're not going to take my son!"

Recovering from the impact of being tossed, Bernard staggered to his feet. As he moved away from the wagon, the girl punched him hard in the back of the head and he grew dizzy falling back onto the wagon, where he decided to stay until he could somehow slip away.

"Five! Five for your moped!"

The once brown young man took a bite from the chicken and began to cry.

"Look what you made me do!"

The girl stood up on her tiptoes and kissed him. The fat lady reached for her hedge clippers. The Harvester brought down his golf club on her head. As they distracted each other, an injured Bernard took this chance to roll from the wagon and run west, hopefully to the edge of the suburbs and the mud and from there, hopefully to Archelon Ranch. It had to be at the edge of the suburbs. It had to be out there somewhere.

Doors opened. Suburbanites in pricy wooly sweaters, moth-eaten suits, or more often no clothes at all, walked outside, knowing that something that wasn't them was out there and seeking, in their addled bundle of instincts, to make it one of them, to play with it until it died or to fuck it bloody and then eat it. He tried to become the houses, the doors, the windows, the couches, the televisions and begged the Objectivity to let him, but it refused. It didn't want to know what it was to be them in spite of the pull in their direction. It would not comply whether it was a matter of survival or not.

He kept running, getting winded, getting weak, knowing that they were behind him and emerging from their fog of Id driven confusion into the realm of predatory impulses. He gave up trying to become anything, until he reached a place where he felt the Objectivity salivating, begging him, whimpering like a puppy or a child. It yanked hard, suddenly understanding an immense experience could be theirs, one so undeniably vast and nuanced that it had to know what it was like.

"How have you lived so long?" it asked him, more a being and less a condition than ever, "how have you lived so long without feeling this? Without being it? How can anything call itself human without knowing? Take it Bernard. You are this."

I am not. You are. I am Bernard. NO! I am Bernard. The Objectivity rebutted, "You are not a Suburbanite, but you *are* this!" The dust tunnel would not spit him out if they got him here. He would never see Archelon Ranch and know the end of suffering. Sooner, or later, he would end up as one of them or food for one of them. He had no choice. I am the Mud.

No you are not. I am the Mud. You cannot be. I am the Mud and you are not the Mud. I am the Mud. The puddle of active mud fought hard for its beingness, but Bernard and the Objectivity hungered so much more deeply for it. You are not the Mud! I am the Mud.

He was confused at being a gilawalrus snatching a child from the top of a lamppost. Then he was confused as he screamed, "No outside food!", pulled a trigger and shot a monkey for eating a grub off itself in the line at the Mall. He was the Mud, wasn't he? The Slaughterer undulated on the stage unloved. A tyrannosaurus gnashed upon a school bus, unmolested by a group of apathetic policemen. There was a strange, old timey street where a fat twenty-something walked home, screamed at by people in passing cars. Two fat middle-aged men argued over a pile of boxes. Homeless people on the street held out empty guitar cases for change that would never be filled. He was the suffering, bubbling to the surface and eating the earth, eating the minds that couldn't understand it.

"Understand," said the suffering, "you must understand."

Archelon Ranch is calling. Archelon Ranch is calling from the center. He reached out for the center as the Objectivity reached for all the suffering around him, all the experiences it could take in and comprehend. I am Bernard and I am at the center. I understand. I am Bernard. The Objectivity had pulled him completely away from the suburbs and the world of places and it yanked him right into the center.

X

This wasn't an adventure. This wasn't a hero's quest for glory, a man's ascension to something greater. This was short, this was ugly. This book killed the man who had the most faith in it and let the one who had the least survive. As I looked on a sign that declared the dull nothing-place past the suburbs "North Enonshire" in bland, Courier font, I realized just how small the book really was. There are people with six hundred pages to count on, six book epics with twists and turns and magnificent vistas, but I wasn't in one of them. I was in a short, ugly, metaphysical mess, by a young author who didn't write big heavy novels nowadays. A bloody tear streaked down the cheek of the sad virgin mary statue that was the closest thing to a person on these dull, silent streets, the closest thing to beauty that rewarded my cruel short trip through the suburbs.

She stood guard over a red, cobblestone path which led up to a white, derelict house. At the end of the path a puddle of gray slush lay on the ground melting, slightly yellowed by the urine of the black and white dog in the front yard. It was smallish but fat, roundheaded, sunken-eyed, tottering on weak legs, begging to be permitted death. It stopped, walked to the same gray slush pile and pissed on it, yellowing it a tiny bit more and then let out an anemic bark. It was joined by a pack of dogs of different breeds, all in similar shape; a pack of beasts bearing only the slightest semblance of life. There was a muffled cry in the distance and they perked up their ears, dutifully following it.

The front lawn didn't look as big as it did from a distance. Spaces were different here, wrong. When I got there it was the size of a small city block. A small blonde child sat there playing with dinosaurs.

"Hello, I'm Clyde," I said, holding out my hand. He didn't take it. A few feet away, a fat, bland looking teenager with dark brown hair and glasses was swinging from a noose tied to an ancient apple tree. The branch collapsed under his weight, he fell right beside the child, who didn't notice at all, then got up, dusted himself off and tied the noose once more. The branch grew back instantly to accommodate him. The front yard should have been enough to tell me not to come closer, but I couldn't resist. If this place could do what the Reverend said it could, I needed it to happen. I walked toward the front porch.

An old man sat there on an overstuffed orange chair. His hair was dark grey, his face gnarled but elfin and his eyes a piercing and judgmental blue.

"Uh uh," he told me, "you don't wanna go in there."

I ignored him and opened the front door, which had a cardboard skeleton awkwardly taped to it, mocking its actual potential for menace, guarding the threshold of this "Narrativist Sacred Site". It didn't look particularly sacred. It looked like I was walking not into a shrine but into a museum of torment. Considering the crappy world around me, I wondered whether Cook spent a lot of time here because if he did my hatred of him wouldn't matter much since he'd beaten me to the punch. I almost tripped over an orange cat in the foyer. It rubbed against me, dripping leaking guts onto my shoe. Cook must love this thing for it to be here, kept in a state like this, so I kicked it as far as I could, giving back a fraction of the pain he'd given me.

When I passed the foyer, suddenly I was nothing, or maybe I was not myself. Objectivity, terrible, virulent Objectivity took over. My ego was lain low by the impression that there was no Clyde. The world was vast and there were many things and many people in it but there was no Clyde. I could not comprehend my hands, my feet, my past. The last feeling that I could say for sure was my own was sympathy for Bernard's struggle with this, the worst of all ailments.

I was choking. There was air around me, but there was none to breathe. The sun wasn't for me, the grass wasn't for me, the moon wasn't for me and the stars only pitied me. Nothing in the world was meant to be enjoyed by me. I loved the beauty of the earth, but it refused to love me back, to say that it was alright to enjoy it. My body was heavy, my face pale, pockmarked and ugly. I had no business here. In spite of myself, I tied the noose to the branch, even knowing that it would simply snap under my weight. The noose didn't matter anyway. Whether I hanged or I didn't, I was still choking. The air smelled of summer strawberries that I would never eat and in the distance I heard laughter at some perfect joke that I couldn't hear. I knew people danced and kissed and cared for each other and I would never have it. Choking, everything was choking, so I had to be done with it. I had to be done with this… I wandered…

Something was wrong with me and I could not tell what it was. I knew that there was supposed to be people around, but I could not find them and it did not concern me. I had my dinosaurs. Shoelaces are hard to tie. Big cars cannot be driven. Sharp things will hurt you. I will stay here where it is soft and comfortable and it doesn't matter what they say about me. It doesn't matter if I draw the pictures right or what peg goes into what hole. It doesn't matter that I don't wash the dishes right or that I can't keep my things in order. I am not stupid. I am special. I am different. I was a poisoned little self playing on the lawn, ignoring all the things that people said about me. I drifted inside the house, glad to no longer be the little boy on the lawn.

There is nothing underneath my skin. There is nothing in me. I am huge, fold upon fold. The flesh, the fat, it covers my eyes and I cannot quite see. I have a mouth leading down a vast hole to another vast hole, a cauldron of empty. I am heavy but I need to be filled. Big round nothing in the middle. The walking zero strains its fragile wobbly meat legs, shuffling on feet I can't even see. The folds grow and grow but there is nothing within. Blob won't even get through the archway. Soon it won't even move. So sweet, but all of it is nothing. The flavors of dust and air are countless but they will never sate. The stomach hangs over my knees and the hole rumbles more. Holes open in the fleshy folds on the side of the head. They call out for more and I oblige them. I do everything they tell me, but they're just holes. Big round nothing. Something else again, please, something else!

Crawling like a snake I ask, "Where are my legs?" There is something in me that makes me stiff and numb. My lungs have no wind, my body has no purpose, no strength. I crawl and crawl and crawl and crawl but I don't know where I'm going. I hear the footfalls of runners, the crack of baseball bats as homeruns scream toward the stratosphere. My nose runs, my throat burns and I'm ready to throw up, rid myself of this poison. I want to get healthy but I'm sick sick sick sick. Even if my legs grew back, even if my posture straightened out, there would still be only sickness in me. Mr. Pandemic, victim of the Me virus.

Sickly nothing. Worthless, broken down cripple. This shell is not me, but it defines me. I am just as sick. The snot, the vomit, the molecules of self evidence of the medical waste that I am. Don't fart, don't sneeze. Enough of you exists already.

Floating in water, I am now three pounds of eelish Cook stretched into the shape of a question mark. Why did you do it? For attention, for love? To make somebody sorry? No water, no tears. I wish I had hands to touch, hands to cut. I wish that I were more than this. There is no future for the drowned, no body for this casket. There are no attendees for this funeral. There are no readers for these poems. The question mark is still not sure it has failed, still not sure its mode of being is the wrong one. It wants the answers it can't get. It wants to hear you're loved, you're famous, you're surrounded by friends. We will accept you, sad or not. It wants the things it cannot have, as all people do, it being want. Answer me, answer me true: do you love me as I love you? Answer me, answer me true: do you love me as I love you?

I try to hold onto myself harder. I cannot stand this. This is not a sacred place. Only sick people could think that the Sad House is sacred and keep it from crumbling. You're sick, Garrett Cook, you're sick! It reached for me and I resisted, and I don't know if I was confusing or strengthening it. The selves interbred. The child rode the question mark and they took off into the air, soaring through a bleeding sky. The fat, having absorbed its arms and legs completely, tried to squeeze under a bathroom door to shit out the poisons in the cripple. This was not poetry. This was not beautiful. The Reverend called this Garrett Cook lord and master, but he was not. The child, on the ground again for some reason, struggled beneath a carpet of fat, the teenager tied the question mark around his neck to hang himself. The dead cats and dogs lap up a trail of the cripple's vomit. The teenager smiles, as if he might make it now. As the question constricts him, he calls out, "Answer me, answer me true, do you love me as I love you?" I had to differentiate. Like the child, I was struggling under the weight of the author's twisted selves, the temptation to give up on life. I cried out, glad to still have a mouth as the abominations absorbed each other.

"Is this sacred to you? Beautiful? Funny? Righteous? Think of what you're doing! Think of what's going on here!"

The selves halt. The question mark lets the teenager breathe, the fat gingerly rolls the little boy onto the lawn, the dogs nuzzle the cripple's face to give him a moment of comfort. This could not be all there was to Garrett Cook. There had to be more. They whispered back and forth and then approached me.

"Nothing fills me," said the fat.

"I am sick," said the cripple.

"I'm not dumb, I'm different," said the child.

"I don't deserve this," said the teenager.

"I'm confused," said the question mark.

"Where are you?" I shouted, "Where are you, Garrett Cook?"

I felt a hand on my shoulder and out of thin air, Bernard appeared beside me. I considered reaching for my gun, but something stopped me. I hoped it wasn't the plot.

"This isn't him," Bernard explained, "not all of him at least. The rest is someplace else. These things are like the mud, they're filth that devours everything."

I hated him even more when he said that, hated him for being here and having answers. These were my questions, I had been forced to live with them and suffer with them as he was named center of the universe. I hoped it was Garrett Cook that held me back, because I wanted to put a bullet in him for every time the Reverend told me I was nothing, every time I thought about Bernard attaining Archelon Ranch while everybody else was trapped in that nightmare jungle of a city. But Garrett Cook wasn't here, so I hurt Bernard instead, the only way I knew for sure I could wreck him.

"He doesn't know how to get there, Bernard. That's why you've had all this trouble, that's why you're here instead of there. There is no Archelon Ranch. He didn't write it and he doesn't know at all where to find it."

Each word wounded me just as much it did him. This world he'd made was one without answers, one where the question mark was king, undisputed, and the Protagonist, the greatest hero there was, couldn't even be himself.

"It's at the center," said Bernard, "I'll find it at the center. You can come too, Clyde."

"I can't and you know it, Bernard. Wouldn't want to because there's nothing to find there."

"Don't say that, Clyde. It's out there, I promise."

I went crazy. I was tired of Narrativist myths and shattered personas, tired of the unfairness of existence. There was nothing but red before my eyes as I screamed. I felt like I was screaming for my whole fucking world.

"Bastard! You fat, depressed, self-loathing bastard! How dare you do this to me! How dare you build a world just to torture people! Who could read this? Who could enjoy this? It isn't fair! Come out and answer me you fat, gutless coward! I'm going to kill you! I'll kill you worse than these things kill themselves! I'll kill you and make it count, too!"

I reached for them with the Objectivity the Sad House had bestowed on me. I wanted to absorb them, bring them together and make them really explode on each other. I think I would have really enjoyed that. But the Objectivity and the mutant selves didn't comply, they simply moved out of the way as the writer Garrett Cook emerged from the doorway of the Sad House. He didn't look as bad as any of those things, nor did he look particularly impressive either, even with the gold tophat he wore for no good reason. He petted the dead black and white dog without fear or disgust, even stopping to hug the pathetic creature.

"I've missed you, girl," were the first words I ever heard out of the mouth of the writer, Garrett Cook. I reached into the backpack for the last of my guns and pointed it at his head.

"Finally! Finally you make yourself accountable! I'm going to love doing this!"

"I came because Bernard called me," he said, looking at me as if I were nothing. No, scratch that. He didn't look *at* me, he looked through me. Sickening. The Deus Ex Machina had come and he was ready to reward Mr. Bigshot-fucking-Protagonist with passage to Archelon Ranch.

"You've been through so much, Bernard. I'm truly sorry." Garrett Cook's head hung in shame.

"He's been through enough? What the hell is wrong with you! He hasn't been through shit! You're dead!"

"I'm not," he replied and yawned for dramatic emphasis. The author was apparently a whole different entity from the thing these creatures made up.

"And why is that?"

"Because you're holding a poodle."

My gun was gone and as he said, I was holding a toy poodle. I felt like I was in an *Abraham the Jellyfish* cartoon.

"I still hate you."

"No, you don't," he retorted with an arrogant smile and apparently tried to do something about it. I say apparently, since in spite of his attempts to rectify it, I still hated him, utterly and passionately, burning with the fire of a thousand exploding stars. He broke a sweat concentrating on his magic trick and as he did, the selves all snickered. The little boy laughed particularly hard. Garrett Cook, puzzled and irritated, shrugged his shoulders in defeat. I felt slightly vindicated.

"Let's go, Bernard," he huffed, taking Bernard's hand to lead him down a gilded road that materialized as the words were spoken. The road seemed to stretch on for miles, in fact it looked as if... I knew it. I laughed derisively.

"That road doesn't end!"

I laughed harder. Squealing like a satisfied monkey. I fell to the ground and rolled around in my smug laughter like a movie tycoon in his money. Garrett Cook ignored me, but Bernard was finding it difficult. Dense as he was, my brother understood. There were tears in his eyes and his face was vermillion. Garrett Cook turned around, retracting the road with a gesture.

"What are you doing?" he screamed at me.

"Nothing," Bernard answered, "he isn't doing anything at all."

"You've been through so much," Garrett Cook repeated, "I'm sorry, Bernard."

I had grown tired of hearing that.

"What about me? Do you know what I've been through?"

There was a peculiar sensation. I felt like somebody was dusting my chromosomes for fingerprints. I felt turned inside out. I thought at that moment that he was going to tear me apart and delete me for being insubordinate. I was ready for it, though. I closed my eyes so I wouldn't have to watch my unmaking. There was nothing to look at when the feeling went away. No comeuppance, oblivion, dissection or tentacle rape, no wild dogs or Suburbanites. Then for a moment, I was not there at all. Completely not there, completely consumed.

Bernard was hugging me, eyes still full of tears. I got the feeling that he was about to do something wonderful, a true act of heroism. And he did. It sticks with me even now.

"I'm sorry, Clyde," he said, "it wasn't fair. I'm sorry for what I did to you."

Bernard became me. He understood me and it was too much for him to bear, too great a strain upon his sheltered conscience. Apologizing was the last thing he ever did before fading into Total Objectivity. I don't miss Bernard much now, since he's omnipresent. I talk to him through my desk lamp sometimes. But right then, my rage toward Garrett Cook erupted worse than ever.

"Why did you do that? Why the fuck would you do that to my brother?"

"Because I like you better."

He was solemn and I could tell he really meant it. With another gesture, he extended the gilded road again and trembling, hesitating, we began to make our way to Archelon Ranch. I could smell perfume, I got visions of perfect maidens, I could hear waves crash and felt the warm guidance of the primordial sea turtles. There was a set of gates just ahead, just ahead and we'd be fine.

But it didn't last long. A mob dressed in white togas had formed. The selves from the Sad House were only part of the crowd that fell upon him like angry suburbanites. I didn't know these people, but the look on Garrett Cook's face registered only fear and not surprise. That's when I figured out who they were. There was his girlfriend, his schoolyard companions, his family, college buddies, faceless people he knew from the internet, fellow writers, his publisher. They each had a knife in their hand but weren't shy about using their teeth on him. There were calls of et tu, et tu, et tu...

He had no limbs when they were done, no eyes, face or organs, only an assortment of scattered gnawed, slashed and shattered parts. The poor son-of-a-bitch. He had sought to make a paradise, had tried to be fair to everyone but he just couldn't. He couldn't even trust himself. I stopped hating him and started pitying him, knowing that the injustice and cruelty wasn't just for us.

I got down on my hands and knees and began to gather every piece I could. I could feel him coming back together as I did. The traitors, confused at what they'd done joined me in this anatomical dig and they were admirable. I wept at how his girlfriend treasured his heart. Someday, someday. Archelon Ranch is calling me. Someday, we'll try again and we'll get there and you'll stay whole, I promise.

About the Author

Garrett Cook is 27. For now. Who knows what will happen in the future? He lives in the Northwest Suburbs of Illinois with his girlfriend of five years. They hope to own property together someday, so tell everybody you know about this book, even people that you don't think will like it very much. He is a member of the Bizarro fiction movement and is the winner of the First Annual Ultimate Bizarro Showdown. His books Murderland Part I: H8 and Murderland Part 2: Life During Wartime have been published by hacker warlord Emperor Needle and his Evil Nerd Empire. He works for them as Sanitizer Overlord, which is every bit as awesome as it sounds. He still feels deeply connected to his past, but would rather it leave him alone. He is prone to strange fancies and dark moods. He is paranoid and a worrier. He is virtually unemployable, but he tries, dammit. He is happy sometimes, he is sad sometimes, he is human all of the time, more so than anything else, so don't judge him as harshly as he does or as Clyde does.

Here is a photo of him at his dark, European, broody best:

http://thegarrettcook.blogspot.com
thecentercannothold@gmail.com

Coming Soon From LegumeMan Books
www.legumeman.com

Dinner Bell for the Dream Worms
by Jason Wuchenich

This debut collection from Jason Wuchenich contains two examples of twisted, subversive fiction - the post apocalyptic hell of 'The Decay Fence' and the flatulent nightmare of 'The Stinky Incubus'. A perfect antidote to good taste.

Coming soon

Alleys
by R. Frederick Hamilton

The followup to R. Frederick Hamilton's very well received 'Spare Key' somehow packs an even more brutal punch. Siction at its finest and most deleriously unpleasant.

Coming in 2010

Merlin's Curse:
The Prolapse Loophole
by The Brothers Gunther

The first installment of a ten part behemoth, penned by LegumeMan founders, the Brothers Gunther. Unstoppably strange

Coming somewhen, somehow

Also Available
www.legumeman.com

A Million Versions of Right
by Matthew Revert

This impossibly warped collection of short fiction has to be read to be believed. The limits of absurdity have been reached and violently destroyed. Guaranteed to melt your brain into pie innards.

Spare Key
by R. Frederick Hamilton

...This was the way it always started. First he would see them and the air would thicken. Then the image of them bound. Then came the screaming and the Red Room would appear with the glittering, new meathook waiting just for them. And there in the Red Room he could play for as long as he wanted...

Coming soon from Evil Nerd Empire
Murderland 2: Life During Wartime – by Garrett Cook

Jeremy and Cass have declared war on the world of Reap, but Jeremy's visions of the Dark Ones still haunt him. The answers are at the mall in Connecticut, where an old friend and some new allies join the battle, like the homeless street preacher General Lud and Inscrutability Jones, the king of the Connecticut underworld. The world of mechanized hatred and bestial violence has a new enemy and his name is Mr. 400, a controversial vigilante that will turn the Reap world upside down in a number of ways. The battle will be long.

www.evilnerdempire.com

www.legumeman.com

CPSIA information can be obtained at www.ICGtesting.com
Printed in the USA
LVOW13s0049091113

360637LV00001B/55/P